Für meinen Schatz

THE OTHER LIFE

THE OTHER LIFE

Susanne Winnacker

First published in Great Britain in 2012 by
Usborne Publishing Ltd
This Large Print edition published 2012
by AudioGO Ltd
by arrangement with
Usborne Publishing Ltd

ISBN: 978 1445 826837

British Library Cataloguing in Publication Data available

Printed and bound in Great Britain by
MPG Books Group Limited

Laughter bubbled out of her.

It shrilled louder the higher she got. I pushed the swing harder, sending Mia soaring into the sky.

'More!'

Tomorrow, my hands would be sore from all the pushing.

Mia's laughter spurred me on. 'Don't let go.'

She'd be hoarse soon.

Laughter and the pale blue sky above us.

I wished all days were like this.

CHAPTER ONE

3 years, 1 month, 1 week and 6 days since I'd seen daylight. One-fifth of my life.

'We've run out of food,' Dad said as he stepped into the doorway of the pantry. He avoided looking at us, especially Mom, ashamed to admit what we'd known for a while. We'd pretended it wasn't happening, but we weren't blind.

Please, not another fight.

Mom looked up from the floor of our improvised kitchen, stopped mopping and set the mop aside. I watched a little puddle of water gathering around it. Her unwashed, blonde hair hung limply down her shoulders and back, and the look of exhaustion on her face made my stomach clench. 'What are you talking about? We should have food for at least another eight months.'

It was impressive how easily the lies slipped from her lips—as if she hadn't noticed. She wiped her hands on her flowery apron—exactly eighty-nine flowers, I'd counted them. She stepped into the pantry. Here it came.

1,139 days since I'd heard the chatter of my friends, since I'd seen the sky.

Hands on hips, Mom glared at Dad, her brows creating a solid line of rising anger. 'We stocked food for four years. You said so yourself.'

Dad sighed. He slumped against one of the shelves and ran a hand through his hair. 'We must have miscalculated. Maybe we ate more than we should have.'

It always began like that: accusations and denial,

followed by screaming and then crying. After that came hours of ignoring each other, and punishing silence. Today was the 996th day they'd spent arguing.

996 out of 1,139. Not a bad rate. Or not good, depending on how you want to look at it. Only four more days and they'd reach 1,000. Maybe some kind of celebration was due. Sometimes I wondered if they even realized how often they shouted at each other. Maybe they didn't care. Or maybe it was their way of killing time.

27,336 hours since I'd smelled freshly cut grass, or eaten a popsicle.

'You calculated the rations! You alone!' Mom pointed an accusing finger at Dad. It shook slightly and a droplet of sweat ran down her temple, shining in the artificial light. The generator for the air conditioning system was running out of energy. It was getting hot. I pedalled a bit faster and the air became cooler.

'You said the food would last for four years. You said so,' Mom said, her face strained. 'Four years!' Her shrill tone made me cringe. Only a matter of seconds before she would burst into tears.

Dad threw up his hands, a look of utter frustration on his face. 'Well, obviously it hasn't. The children have grown. They needed more food than we could have foreseen!' His voice rose. It filled the small space and bounced off the sterile white walls.

1,640,160 minutes since I'd run, since the wind had tousled my hair, since I'd seen any other person apart from my family.

'Your father died six months ago. His ration should have provided enough food to make up for that!' Mom shouted.

4

Grandma winced, but she didn't stop knitting. She seldom did. Her hands moved even faster, the knitting needles clicking together while she did one stitch after the other.

Click. Click.

If we'd taken as much food with us as Grandma had taken yarn, this argument wouldn't have happened. There was enough yarn for a decade in the pantry. My eyes flitted to our top-opening freezer—Grandpa's last resting place. Until three months ago, we'd stored our frozen food next to him. I shuddered and pedalled faster, ignoring the burning in my legs. Sweat trickled down my calves.

98,409,600 seconds since I'd felt sun on my skin.

98,409,602 seconds since the heavy, steel door had fallen shut and sealed us off from the world. Imprisoned us.

'This is our last can of food!' Mom held up a small silver tin of corned beef. 'How long do you think it will feed six people? How long? Why didn't you say anything before? You should have warned us!'

Next came the crying. No doubt.

Mom must have noticed our lack of food weeks ago. Even Mia had asked why the shelves were empty. Mom was only looking for a reason to fight with Dad—it'd been like that for months.

'It's not my fault!' Dad bellowed. 'Why didn't you take a look in the pantry? If you stopped scrubbing the counters and floors every bloody minute of the day, you would have realized it on your own!'

He stormed out of the pantry, but there was nowhere he could go. He stopped in front of the furthest wall—barely ten metres away. His shoulders shook and his right hand rose to hide his eyes. I'd have bet on Mom, she usually cried first. And she

5

was a loud crier. She didn't even try to hide it from us.

Before life in the bunker, I'd never seen Dad cry. Now it was a common occurrence—generally about twice a week, but Mom was still in the lead when it came to hysterical breakdowns. Perhaps a few more weeks and it would be a tie. If we were still alive.

Mom stood in the doorway of the pantry, the tin of corned beef in her outstretched palms like a sacred artefact. Her lips were pressed together and tears rolled down her pale cheeks. Her skin looked like ash—no fresh air and nothing but artificial light did that to you.

The television flickered because I'd stopped pedalling, and a moment later the screen went black. Bobby turned around and scowled at me. He took out an earplug and opened his mouth. I shook my head and gave him a warning look. His eyes flitted over to Dad, then Mom, and his brows pulled down in a frown.

'Bobby?' Mia whined as she pulled at his sleeve. Disappointment filled her round face, because Ariel, the Little Mermaid, had just disappeared from the screen. Bobby wrapped his arm around her shoulders and turned her so she wouldn't see Mom and Dad arguing. Again. Then he raised his eyebrows at me in a silent demand.

Usually, I didn't do what he told me. He was younger than me by two years and was supposed to listen to me—though he rarely did.

I returned my feet to the pedals and began cycling. Ariel reappeared on screen, happily swimming with her little fishy friends through the ocean. It had been so long since I'd eaten fish; though it was better not to mention that to Mia—she loved Ariel's

6

undersea kingdom.

I couldn't remember how the ocean smelled or how it felt to walk barefoot on the beach, the sand between my toes. I didn't even know if any of my friends were still alive. What had they looked like? They were nothing but a fading memory. I swallowed the lump in my throat and pedalled as fast as I could.

Mom still hadn't moved from the pantry. 'That's all we have,' she whispered, looking down at the tin like it was our tombstone. Dad didn't turn away from the wall to look at her. His shoulders had stopped shaking, though. Mom lifted her face and stared at me. Her tears didn't stop. Then she looked at Bobby and Mia, who were immersed in the movie that they'd seen too many times before. Bobby hated *The Little Mermaid*—he only watched it for Mia's sake.

The tin fell to the carpet with a dull thud. It rolled a few centimetres before it halted on its side. Every inch of this carpet was familiar to me. Every stain, every blemish. I looked up from the ground. Mom's hands shook. 'That's all we have left.' Her eyes were wide as she clapped a hand over her mouth. It did nothing to stifle the sobs.

My legs slowed. The TV screen flickered and I accelerated once more. Dad turned his head slightly to look over his shoulder at Mom. When sobs turned into gasps for air, I stopped pedalling and jumped off the bike. Dad and I reached Mom a second before her legs gave way.

'Mom, look at me.' I took her hand and squeezed, while Dad lowered her to the ground. Her eyes flickered between Dad and me.

'Honey, breathe in and out,' Dad instructed, but Mom didn't seem to hear. Her gasps grew desperate and pained, her eyes frantic.

Eight months ago Mom's asthma medication had run out.

Tears burned in my eyes and I blinked them back. 'Mom.' I cupped her cheeks and forced her to look at me. 'Breathe with me, Mom.' I took a deep breath and let it out, my lips forming an exaggerated 'O'. 'In and out, Mom. In and out.' Her eyes finally focused. She attempted to suck in air, her chest heaving. I nodded and showed her again. 'In and out.' Her breath was rattling, but at least she was breathing. Dad held her hand, their fight forgotten, and stared at us. His eyes were red, his cheeks sunken in, his skin too pale. I couldn't remember when I'd last seen him eat something. He was starving himself for our sake. I looked back at Mom and repeated the breathing—in and out. In and out.

Grandma hadn't stopped knitting.

Click. Click.

She hadn't even looked up.

Click. Click.

'There's still room next to my Edgar.' Grandma's harsh Bavarian accent cut through the room. Every pair of eyes in the bunker flitted to the freezer. Every pair except for Mia's.

Thank God.

As far as she knew, Grandpa had spent the last six months happily in heaven and not rock-hard next to our frozen peas. Mom's weak smile faltered and she swallowed visibly.

'Grandpa Edgar?' Mia turned, her eyes wide with curiosity. Grandma looked up from the half-finished scarf, but she didn't stop knitting.

Click. Click.

'Yes, your grandpa, of course.' The clicking of the

8

needles filled the room.

Click. Click.

'Do you want me to show you?'

The vein in Dad's temple began throbbing. A warning sign. 'Be quiet, for God's sake!' he said under his breath. He never talked to Grandma like that.

'I don't think we've taught you to be disrespectful, son.' Grandma's voice remained a whisper. She didn't stop knitting.

Click. Click.

Mia's curious blue eyes moved between Dad and Grandma. 'You said Grandpa was in heaven. Will we visit Grandpa in heaven?'

Mom turned and walked into the pantry, closing the curtain behind her. It didn't muffle her sobs. Dad's hands were balled fists as he glared at Grandma. Bobby sat down on the exercise bike and began pedalling, his eyes closed. His jaw was clenched so tightly it looked painful.

I took Mia's hand and led her towards the kitchen table, where I sank down on a chair and lifted her onto my lap. 'Will we visit Grandpa in heaven?' she asked again, looking up at me with her clear blue eyes. I smiled. The muscles around my mouth felt like they might cramp from the effort. 'No, Mia.'

Her smile fell and she pouted. 'Why not?'

'It's not time yet.'

I hadn't been to a party yet, had never dyed my hair, never kissed a boy. There were so many 'nevers'.

Dad glanced at me with approval and set his mouth in a determined line before he nodded, obviously pleased with my answer. I set Mia down and gave her a small clap on her backside. 'Now, go

9

watch Ariel.'

Mia's head whirled towards the TV that had flickered back to life and she hurried over to her earlier spot on the ground. She dropped down on her bottom, already glued to Ariel with rapt attention. Every member of this family could recite the entire movie by heart. If I closed my eyes, the movie played out in my mind, only disturbed by the sound of Grandma's knitting.

Click. Click.

Mom hadn't emerged from the pantry yet, but her sobs had subsided. Or she'd finally found a way to muffle the noise. Probably the latter.

Grandma was knitting her sixtieth scarf. Bobby pedalled like a maniac. Both were busy ignoring Mom. Sometimes I felt like the only adult in the bunker. I ran a hand through my hair and winced when my fingers met knots. My hair felt dull. We'd run out of shampoo and conditioner fourteen months ago. Our soap supply had lasted till three weeks ago. A short shower every three days was all our water supplies allowed anyway. Sometimes the smell of sweat and Bobby's feet became unbearable, but there was nowhere we could go.

I picked up a strand between my thumb and forefinger and inspected it. My red hair had been shiny once.

1,139 days ago I'd stopped caring about such things.

I dropped the strand and picked up the tin of corned beef. All that was left. It was obvious it would never feed six people—not even three. Actually, I doubted it would be enough to fill the void in my stomach alone.

I lifted a pot from the cupboard, filled it with

water and turned on the smaller burner before I set it down. The water only took a few minutes before it began to boil. After opening the tin, I dumped the corned beef in.

'What are you doing?' Dad came up next to me and peeked in.

Stirring the brew with a wooden spoon, I looked up at him. 'Making soup.'

His eyes lit up with understanding. 'You are a clever girl, Sherry.' He stroked my cheek and gave me a smile. Sometimes he still treated me like a little girl, as if he hadn't noticed how I'd taken the role of an adult recently—or maybe he'd chosen to ignore it. From the corner of my eye, I saw the curtain being pulled back. Mom stepped out of the pantry, her face cleaned of tears. She approached Dad and me with an embarrassed smile.

'I'll set the table,' she announced. She grabbed soup bowls and spoons, and put them on the table. Dad hesitated briefly before he went to help her. I looked away when he wrapped his arms around her waist and murmured something into her ear. Privacy was almost impossible in the bunker.

I stared down at the pot of reddish-brown brew. It looked like dog food.

1,139 days ago I wouldn't have eaten it. But that was a long time ago.

Now, I couldn't wait.

Everyone settled around the table, even Grandma. The smell of something to eat—no matter how gross—drew her in like a moth to the light. Food was the only thing that could stop her from knitting continuously. In the last months of Grandpa's struggle against cancer, she'd begun to knit obsessively—it was occupational therapy for her.

Since his death, she'd barely stopped.

While the clicking of the needles seemed to calm Grandma, it was slowly driving the rest of my family crazy. Right now, the *click-click* felt like the countdown to something. Time was running out.

Click. Click.

I grabbed the pot and put it in the middle of the table. A scoop for each person. Not much.

Dad opened his mouth—in protest, I guess—when I filled his soup bowl. I ignored him, and silence settled over us as we ate what little we had.

Dad didn't pick up his spoon at first. I glanced up and pleaded with him with my eyes: *Stop sacrificing yourself.* He dipped his head and stared at the soup. Then, finally, he began eating, guilt radiating from his face.

Dinner took us less than two minutes. Mia was the last to finish. She put down her spoon and looked at the empty plate with so much longing that I wished I'd given my soup to her.

Minutes dragged by in silence. Not the silence that surrounds you like a warm blanket, but a silence that threatens to crush you.

Longing glances were cast at empty plates, resigned glances at the empty pantry.

1,139 days since I'd seen daylight.

Only 2 minutes since we'd run out of food.

The kitchen smelled of lebkuchen and apple pie. Grandma formed the dough into small crescents for the vanille kipferl.

Perfect.

I dipped my finger into the cream-cheese creme, brought it to my lips. The sugary taste filled my mouth, coating my tongue. The best pie filling in the world. Home-made. Grandma would never allow convenience food into her house.

Just one more taste.

'Sherry, honestly, don't eat it, you'll be sick tomorrow.'

Nothing but a rumour Grandma spread so she had enough creme to bake her Bavarian apple pie.

'I'm just testing the quality.'

She tried to look disapproving, but pushed the bowl in my direction.

'One more taste, then wash your hands. And don't tell your mother.' She smiled at me conspiratorially.

The cream-cheese creme melted on my tongue. The best taste in the world.

CHAPTER TWO

My eyes were closed as I listened to the sounds around me.

Click. Click. Grandma's knitting.

Swoosh and the occasional click of a button. Dad trying to communicate via his radio receiver.

A long sigh. Mom losing her patience.

No chirping birds, no wind rustling the trees. No diversion. Never.

I opened my eyes and stared at the white ceiling. There was a tiny spot just above my head where Dad had swatted a fly a few days after we locked the door. Often I'd spent hours just staring at it. I rolled onto my side, facing the room. Dad sat at his desk with the radio receiver. Microphone in hand, he turned knobs and pressed buttons with a look of despair. I'd seen that look so often recently. It was carved into his face—ever since we'd run out of food. My stomach clenched and unclenched, but the hollow feeling remained.

'George. Richard here. George, are you there?' Dad asked.

Mia snuggled closer to me. Her eyes were closed and her red hair was all over the place, her curls twisted and knotted. She'd gotten used to sleeping next to me since we'd started sharing a bed 1,141 days ago.

A long time.

We didn't even have to share a bed any more— not since Grandpa had died and Grandma had decided to sleep sitting on the sofa—but Mia refused to sleep on her own. She'd wake as soon as I did, her warm body pressed against mine, easing the crushing feeling of hunger. Her warmth seemed to fill the void. Mia was tough, much tougher than most kids her age. Not a single word of complaint had left her mouth over the last few days. She'd lost a lot of weight—whenever I lifted her or she sat on my lap it was unmistakable. It worried me more than my own weight loss and stomach ache did. She was the baby of this family and I wanted to protect her.

'What time is it?' I asked into the silence, stroking Mia's hair. From my spot on the bed, I couldn't see our sole functioning clock.

'What does it matter?' Bobby's voice was muffled by his pillow, only his dishevelled blond hair peeking out.

'I want to know.'

'Why?' Bobby lifted his head and glared at me. 'It's not as if you've got a date. It's not as if we could do anything! And we don't even have food. We're all going to die.' He buried his face in the pillow once more. I chose to stay silent.

Bobby was in one of his depressive moods. Since he'd turned thirteen a few weeks ago, his mood swings had gotten worse.

Two days ago we'd run out of food. How much longer until we'd be too weak to move? Or until we'd start gnawing on each other? The thought nearly made me laugh. Maybe I was going crazy.

Food. I'd have given anything for a bite of apple. A steak. A s'more. I could almost taste it—the smoky crust and creamy belly of the marshmallow. The crunch of the cracker, the chocolate melting on my tongue. A taste of everything that once was, everything I missed. So sweet.

I pushed the images out of my head. The pain in

16

my stomach was getting too much. My tongue felt as if it was covered with fuzz.

'George, please answer.' Dad held the mic in a tight grip. George Smith had been his best friend since high school.

'He won't answer,' Mom said from her spot on the sofa. 'Nobody will.' Her blonde hair was a mess and her cotton nightgown was full of holes. Nobody would see her anyway, so why bother dressing up?

Grandma sat next to her, knitting.

Click. Click.

I remembered times when Grandma had read books to us, sung with us and baked Bavarian apple pies.

'George? Christine?' Dad's voice got quieter.

Still no answer.

George and Christine Smith were our next-door neighbours, or had been. Their daughter Isabel was my best friend.

1,141 days since I'd seen Izzy. Though her chatty nature sometimes drove me crazy, I'd have given anything to hear one of her excited rambles about her favourite band or the new cute boy. I missed her so much.

'George? Christine? Anyone? Please answer.' Dad buried his face in his palms.

2 months since our last contact with George, Christine and Izzy. Or anyone else, come to that.

63 long days.

'I can't do this any more!' Dad dropped the mic and jumped up. His chair toppled over, and we all stared at him. It was a shock to see him suddenly so animated.

'I won't sit here and wait for us to starve to death.'

I sat up, ignoring Mia's mumbles of protest and

her small hand clutching at my top. Even Grandma had stopped knitting to stare at Dad.

Mom rose from the sofa. 'What are you talking about?'

Dad didn't reply. He walked towards the pantry and emerged after a moment with a shotgun and his police pistol. He stuffed the smaller weapon into a holster that he'd put on his hip.

'Richard?' Mom's voice shook as she walked towards him. I got out of bed. Even Bobby sat up.

'I'm going to leave this damn bunker and find food. I won't watch my family starve.'

Bobby glanced at me, his eyebrows arched in a silent question mark. I shrugged—I didn't know what had gotten into Dad. Mom's chin began to tremble. Any moment now, tears would flow. 'You know what they said when the rabies broke out. We should hide in a shelter and not come out until they'd gotten the mutation under control. They said we should wait until the military told us it was safe to come out. Have you forgotten about the warnings?'

Dad laughed bitterly. 'The military stopped broadcasting almost three months ago, and even before that they sent us the same warning for over a year. It was just a damn recording telling us the same thing over and over again. Do you really think they are suddenly going to start giving us new information?'

Mom swallowed. She shook her head. Dad was right, of course. We hadn't gotten any news for over a year. Actually, the only thing the military had ever broadcast was a warning not to leave our bunkers. No updates. And the voice had come from a stupid recording. Maybe there was no one left out there to broadcast live. I forced the thought out of my head.

18

'The government is the reason that we're living like this. We're on our own. Nobody's going to come and save us. Either I go out there, see what's happening and find food, or we'll starve to death in this bunker.'

Mom shook her head slowly and grabbed his arm. 'You don't know what's still out there. Don't you remember what they said in the warnings? Those people with rabies might still be running loose. Crazy people.'

'I've got a gun. I'm capable of defending myself.'

Mom looked at him pleadingly, her hands clutching his arm, her knuckles white.

'Honey, we'll all die if I don't leave this bunker and find food,' Dad said, his gaze imploring.

Mom closed her eyes and gave a small nod. 'I know.'

Dad smiled and gave her a kiss.

1,141 days since I'd seen the sky, since I'd counted clouds.

A jolt of excitement went through me. My decision was made. 'I'll come with you.'

'No.'

I scrambled for my clothes and pulled them on over the shorts and top I'd slept in. Jeans and a long-sleeved shirt would be okay—it was summer outside. At least I hoped it was.

Dad shook his head. 'Sherry, I said no.'

No? Did he think he could forbid me this after everything I'd done? I'd spent the last few months being the grown-up in this damn bunker because he and Mom had been too busy fighting.

'Dad, you can't go alone. If you get injured, there'll be no one to help you. It's the basic rule of survival training—don't go anywhere alone, always

19

go in pairs. That's what *you* and Grandpa taught us.'

Grandpa had hammered those rules into Dad, and later into Bobby and me. He'd read dozens of books about people who'd survived in the jungle, desert, snow and God knows where else. *Humans cannot survive more than three weeks without food.* I could almost hear him say it.

'If someone should go with your dad, it's me,' Mom said, but her face was fearful. She wouldn't stop me, it was clear.

'What about your asthma? And someone needs to stay here with Grandma, Mia and Bobby.'

Mom frowned. Her eyes darted around the room. 'It's too dangerous. You're just a child.' I opened my mouth to protest but she went on, 'What if something happened to you? I can't lose both of you.'

'Mom, we're just looking for food. Nothing's going to happen.'

I'd convinced her, it was obvious. Bobby crossed his arms in front of his chest. 'I should go with Dad, not you. I can take care of myself; you're a girl.'

I rolled my eyes at him. 'I'm two years older than you, plus Dad took me to the shooting range, and hunting, so I know how to handle a gun.'

Bobby opened his mouth to make a probably not-so-witty comment, but Dad held up a hand. 'Enough.'

All eyes were on him.

'Sherry has a point. I shouldn't go alone and she's our best choice.'

Bobby's shoulders slumped. I had to restrain a smile.

1,141 days since I'd seen daylight, smelled fresh air, felt the wind tousle my hair.

Dad grabbed his jacket and put it on. 'Take your coat with you.'

I nodded while I slipped into Mom's old sneakers. Putting a coat on—also Mom's, it was the only one that fitted me now—I walked towards Dad. He stood in front of the wooden steps that led up to the steel door keeping us safe from whatever was outside. Mom, Bobby and Mia followed behind us. Grandma kept knitting and didn't look up.

Click. Click.

'Be careful and stay close to your dad, and listen to what he says—'

'Mom, don't worry. I'll be fine. *We'll* be fine.'

She didn't look convinced but she gave me a faint smile and hugged me tightly. Eventually her hold loosened. She turned to Dad and kissed him. 'Take good care of her—and come back soon.' There was a quiver in her voice.

'We will,' he promised. He looked eager—he was just as keen as I was to get out.

I hugged Mia and Bobby—despite Bobby's feeble protests—before following Dad up the steps. We stopped in front of the steel door. My hands felt clammy—this was it. Mom climbed up too and halted behind me. Her presence gave me courage for the first time in months, probably years. Dad opened the three locks and pulled. With an ear-splitting creak, the door opened. I held my breath, expecting something to pounce.

Nothing happened.

Warm air pushed against me and filled my lungs. It was stuffy and stale, and I broke out in a sweat. Dad stepped cautiously through into the hallway of our house. His knuckles white as he gripped the shotgun, he checked the corridor, gesturing for me to wait. Then he disappeared from view. After a moment, he returned. 'It's okay. You can come out.'

21

Freedom.

Dad turned to Mom. 'Stay in the bunker. If we haven't returned by tomorrow, grab the other gun in the pantry. Take my mother, Mia and Bobby with you, and try to find other people.'

Mom nodded, tears welling in her eyes as she closed the heavy door. I heard a low clunk—the sound of the deadlock on the other side. Taking a deep breath, I turned away from the bunker.

'Here.' Dad handed me the pistol and holster. 'Do you still remember how to fire at a target?'

I hesitated. Did I? I wasn't sure. Dad and Grandpa had taken me to the shooting range more times than I could count. They'd even let me fire at clay pigeons to improve my aim and it had paid off. I'd been good, very good—but that was long ago. What if I'd forgotten all they'd taught me?

He smiled and grabbed the pistol to show me how to release the safety catch and how to take aim. I hoped we wouldn't need any weapons—but when he handed the gun back to me, I grasped it tightly.

'Stay behind me,' he instructed in a firm tone. I hadn't seen him in stern fatherly mode for a while. A few years ago, it would have annoyed me. Now? Not so much. I'd missed this side of him. He held the shotgun in both hands and walked down the hall. My gun hand shook as I followed him. Soft light filtered into the corridor. Daylight—not the artificial glare I was used to. I blinked. My eyes needed to get used to the natural light, but it felt so good. I could feel a smile tugging at my lips.

I peeked into the living room. Nothing had changed since I'd last seen it. Even Muffin's scratching post was where we'd left it. If I closed my eyes I could see him lounging on the highest

22

platform, meowing to get attention. I wished the soldiers hadn't scared him off. Had he come back after we'd gone into the bunker and wondered where we were? How long had he waited before he'd given up?

Only the layer of dust on every surface indicated the time that had passed. The photo of Izzy and me in our ridiculous Halloween costumes was covered with it. We were grinning like Cheshire cats, arms wrapped around each other. The last Halloween before we went into the bunker.

1,388 days ago.

The taste of Grandma's pumpkin pie. The eerie glow of the jack-o'-lanterns we'd carved with Izzy's mom. The scent of candles and burgers from the grill. Still vivid in my mind.

'Sherry, come on.' Dad was already at the front door.

Sunlight streamed through the windows, though it was dimmed by grime covering the glass. It looked like soot—as if there had been a fire or explosion nearby.

'Sherry.' Dad's voice was full of impatience—and a hint of anxiety. I hurried to his side.

'Have you seen the windows?'

He nodded, with a grim expression, and took the car key from a hook on the wall.

'What does—'

He interrupted me. 'I don't know. We should hurry. We need to see if the neighbours have left their bunkers, and we need to get something to eat.'

He unlocked and pulled at the front door. The hinges screeched in protest. The wood sounded as though it was going to splinter.

'The door's warped. Probably the heat,' Dad said.

23

He yanked, and it swung open.

Warm summer air filled my lungs. Despite the soot on the windows, the air didn't smell of smoke. It smelled fresh, but different to how I remembered it—not as sweet, not as reviving. Maybe my memory was playing tricks on me. After life in the bunker, I'd expected more—a moment of 'wow'.

Dad and I stepped out of the house and shut the door. Sun rays warmed my body and I closed my eyes.

'Sherry!'

My eyes shot open.

Dad shook his head, a deep frown on his face. 'What were you thinking? Don't close your eyes. You must stay alert.'

He stepped from the porch. I followed and looked to my right. The houses looked the same as they always had—Izzy's house was just how I remembered it. Well, almost how I remembered it. The outside was covered with soot and surrounded by high bushes and weeds. The street, once noisy with playing children and busy neighbours, was deserted. We were the only people around, and it was silent. Eerily silent.

Maybe Izzy and her parents were still in their shelter. 'Dad, do you—' I turned my head to look at him and my mouth went dry.

Oh my God.

From where we stood, we could look down over parts of Los Angeles—or what was left of it. Like broken stalagmites, the shattered skyscrapers rose into the sky. Burst windows split the light into thousands of fragments.

'Dad?' My voice shook. 'What happened?' I swallowed.

24

He looked at me, his face blank. 'There must have been a bombardment.'

'Why didn't we hear anything?' I couldn't pull my eyes from the remains of my hometown, from the terrifying beauty of it.

'The bunker is soundproof.' He frowned and shook his head. 'Do you remember the earthquake shortly after we went into hiding?'

I nodded. Then it dawned on me. 'It wasn't an earthquake, right?'

Dad ran a hand through his red hair. 'God, what have they done?' he muttered.

'Who did this? What do you mean?' I asked in a whisper, panic tightening my throat. Who would drop bombs on a town full of people?

'I don't know.' He shook his head. 'I just don't know.'

'Why didn't the military tell us? And where is everyone?' I scanned our surroundings. Maybe they were still hiding like us. But hadn't they run out of food too?

Dad sighed. 'I just don't know, Sherry. We'll have to look around.' He walked across our lawn. The grass reached my thighs, and the neighbours' lawns didn't look much better. The blades of grass rustled as our steps parted them. Nobody had mowed here for years. What if we were the only people still alive?

I felt cold despite the sunshine. We arrived at Izzy's front door. Dad didn't bother to knock—he turned the handle and the door opened.

He glanced at me, his eyes flitting to my pistol. He lifted his shotgun and kicked the door wide, so we could look into the hall. Dust particles swirled in the air, tickling my nose. I held my gun with both hands. My heart was pounding wildly. Dad moved forwards,

25

glancing around. 'George?' His call sliced through the silence.

No reply.

I followed a couple of metres behind him as he walked to the back of the house and into their garden where the bunker was. Dad and George had helped each other building the bunkers—they'd been safety fanatics. Mom and Christine had always made fun of them. They'd laughed together about their 'survivalist men'.

The iron doors were wide open, resting on the grass. Dad peeked into the bunker, then his shoulders slumped. 'It's deserted.'

*   *   *

We searched every cupboard in the house for something to eat, but found nothing. After that, we went through some of the neighbours' houses further up the road—all deserted. We knew most people had been forced to search for shelter in one of the public bunkers in Los Angeles and its suburbs. Everyone had thought it would take only a few days or weeks until the rabies was contained. The government had said so. They had promised.

Only a few days, weeks at the most. It made me want to laugh. More like 1,141 days, and counting.

Why had they even bothered broadcasting their stupid warnings? Once, when they were fighting, Dad had told Mom that the government didn't care about us and probably just wanted to keep us in our bunkers so we never found out how they'd messed up. What if he had been right after all? What if the government hadn't wanted us to find out that they'd failed to contain the rabies, that they'd chosen to

26

bomb an entire city without success? My stomach clenched at the thought.

Most of the other bunkers we discovered were vacant. We found only one that was still closed, but nobody reacted as we knocked and shouted.

We walked down the other side of the street. The heat had cracked the concrete and, with nobody to take care of it, grass was growing out of the cracks. My stomach growled. What if we didn't find food and had to return to the bunker without anything? If the worst came to the worst, we'd just have to hunt some game, or a stray dog or cat.

Dad halted without warning and I almost bumped into him.

Two dead bodies lay on a lawn. I stumbled backwards.

They were mangled and looked as if an animal had ripped chunks out of them. Their skin looked marbled and their bellies were bloated, but maggots hadn't yet hatched. The bodies looked kind of fresh, as if these people had died not long ago. Their flesh wasn't parched from the sun like it would have been after days of exposure.

I barely recognized the bodies as two of our neighbours. Husband and wife. I didn't know their names, but I'd seen them a million times—they'd always been really friendly. Even in death, their widened, lifeless eyes reflected shock.

A hiss escaped one of the bodies as gas fought its way out. The stench was horrible—sweet, rotten and acid all at the same time. I retched and clapped a hand over my mouth. Dad grabbed my arm and pulled me away.

'What happened to them?' I whispered.

Dad's face looked grave. He'd known them better

than me. 'It looks like something attacked them.'

'Some*thing*?' I peeked up at him.

He looked at me with a pained expression. 'It looks like an animal did it. Only I don't know any wild animals in the area that would do something like that. Bobcats and coyotes might feed on humans, but they wouldn't just rip their victims apart randomly.'

I swallowed down the lump rising in my throat. 'Who did it then?'

'I don't know, Sherry.'

He was lying.

'Do you...do you think a human did it?' The thought made me sick. Before the government had ordered everyone to hide in the bunkers, there were rumours about lots of murders in the area. Brutal murders.

Dad didn't reply, but his lips pulled into a tight line. That was all the answer I needed. We both knew the bodies looked like they'd been attacked not long ago. So whatever had murdered them was probably still roaming around *now*.

I glanced over my shoulder as we walked back up to our car in the driveway, but I didn't see anything.

'Sherry?'

I turned around.

A thick layer of soot covered the car, so it looked black instead of grey.

'Help me clean the windshield,' Dad said. He looked around for something he could use. I pushed my sleeve over my hand and started scrubbing the glass. Dad stared, then he did the same. After a few minutes, I could see inside the car.

Dad pulled the key from the back pocket of his jeans and unlocked it. The door creaked when he

28

pulled it open.

'Perhaps we should drive around the area. We might find other people. Maybe even some food.'

Dad's gaze was directed at the remains of Los Angeles. Sometimes it flickered to where the bodies lay, though they were too far away now to see more than just their outlines.

A roar rang in the silence.

I jumped and almost dropped the pistol. With shaking fingers, I released the safety catch and raised the weapon. Dad had lifted his shotgun and was searching our surroundings. The roar had sounded like an animal, only I couldn't think of an animal that made a noise like that.

'Get into the car.' Dad sounded calm but his eyes couldn't hide his panic.

I was paralysed—my legs, my entire body, numb. As if it wasn't even there, as if *I* wasn't there. Gone like everyone else. Iciness crawled into my toes, up my legs and spread into every fibre of me.

'Sherry, get in the damn car!'

This time my body did as it was told. I pulled open the door and slipped into the passenger seat. With a shaky hand, I jerked the door shut. The noise made me jump again. Dad slid behind the steering wheel, closed his door and put the shotgun between his legs. It took him three tries before he got the key into the ignition.

Another roar broke the silence, closer this time.

The pistol resting on my lap, I looked out of the side window. There was nothing. I turned. Something flashed in the corner of my eye. I wrenched my head back round and stared. Something had moved. A shadow. Where was it?

Maybe I'd imagined it.

Dad started the engine, but it died almost instantly. 'What about the others? Should we warn them?'

Dad shook his head. He turned the key again. Nothing this time. A dead click under the bonnet. 'No, they're safe in the bunker. As long as they stay there, everything will be fine. We're going to search for food and maybe for other survivors, and then we'll head back. If we're home before tomorrow, your mother won't have any reason to leave.'

Dad opened the door and got out. Without thinking, I gripped my gun and prepared to shoot if anything tried to attack. It was an automatic response. Grandpa would have been proud.

As soon as Dad lifted the hood of the car, he was hidden from my view. I rocked back and forth on my seat, glancing out of the side window. There was nothing.

Finally Dad snapped the hood shut and walked back to the driver's side. I let out a slow breath. He slipped into the car and closed the door, then turned the key in the ignition again. This time the engine roared to life and Dad pulled the car out of the driveway. He glanced at the fuel gauge—we were almost out of gas.

As our home became a distant silhouette, I couldn't shake off the growing feeling that someone—or something—was watching us.

I made my way across the beach to where the waves touched the sand.

Wind blew my hair all over the place. Relief from the summer heat. I looked over my shoulder at the footprints I'd left behind. Another wave erased every trace of them.

As if I'd never been there.

The next wave rolled towards me. Cold water clawed at my skin.

My family lounged in the shade of a parasol. Dad had the newspaper in front of him. He hadn't put it down all day.

I wished I could ignore the front page with its glaring headline announcing a new curfew after the latest rise in attacks. I wished this wasn't the last day of summer.

Closing my eyes, I brought the popsicle to my lips. The sour taste of lime exploded on my tongue and seemed to fill every part of my body with a new energy.

It tasted like summer.

CHAPTER THREE

Los Angeles' suburbs were deserted. No traffic. No smog. No people.

The sun was shining and it was getting warmer by the minute. It should have been a beautiful day.

Los Angeles had been full of life. Venice Beach with its bold skaters, its crazy tattoo artists, and girls in micro-bikinis. Or the Walk of Fame, with its mass of tourists stumbling over their own feet to take a photo of every star.

This city wasn't Los Angeles. This city was dead, like the ghost town in the Mojave Desert we'd visited a few years back. It was like a corpse, sucked dry of any energy. A few birds sat on the pavement, and I saw a cat scurrying through the broken window of a shop—but they were the only signs of life. Where had everyone gone? Were they still underground, starving to death? Too afraid to leave their shelter? My breath caught in my throat.

There were more weeds and grass peeking through the cracks in the concrete, and soot and dirt covering shop windows. Cars were parked in driveways and at the roadside, waiting for their owners. Goosebumps rose on my skin.

Dad was silent throughout the drive. We were heading towards the grocery store where our family used to shop. I could still remember the route and yet it was nothing like before. The silhouette of a destroyed Los Angeles hovered in the distance. I leaned my head against the sun-warmed window.

There wasn't a single car on the freeway. I did a double take. A group of wild boars crossed the street in the distance. Wild boars in the city? They used to avoid humans. I wrapped my arms around my chest. What if we were the only survivors?

The building with huge Walmart lettering came into view and Dad pulled off the freeway. Bombs must have hit this part of the city—so many houses had collapsed and wooden boards and huge chunks of concrete littered the streets.

Someone had sprayed *Road to perdition* in huge black letters on the facade of one of the buildings. It was the only sign of human life.

'Where are they all? Millions of people can't have disappeared, can they?' I looked at Dad.

He kept his eyes on the road, then glanced at me briefly. 'Maybe they're hiding. Maybe Los Angeles and its suburbs have been declared a restricted area.'

'But why has no one told us? What if everybody's gone? What if they're all dead?' My voice shook and I could feel tears building.

Dad prepared to answer, but then he closed his mouth and frowned as if he was considering his reply. He let out a sigh. 'I don't think that Los Angeles is necessarily indicative of how the rest of the country looks. The rabies had only spread through parts of Canada and the south-west when we went into the shelter. The military should have managed to destroy the virus before it could get any further.'

'But what if they didn't succeed? What if it spread all over the world?'

Dad shook his head. 'No.' He paused. 'No, that isn't possible.' He sounded uncertain and that didn't help to soothe my worries: the recorded message blaring out the same warning for years, deserted

34

streets, no sign of other people. Panic rose up in my throat.

'How do you know? Maybe they're all dead!' I could hear my voice becoming hysterical.

Dad pulled into the Walmart parking lot and stopped the engine before he turned to me. He put a hand on my shoulder and squeezed gently. 'Sherry, there are...there *were* six billion people on this planet. They aren't all dead. It just seems like we're the only people because Los Angeles is such a mess. We'll look for food and then we'll try to find out what's happened and where everybody's gone.' He smiled. 'Okay?' His hand shook when he pulled the key from the ignition.

I took a deep breath. 'Okay.'

Nothing was okay, and we both knew it.

'Good.' He let go of my shoulder and opened the driver's door, checking our surroundings before he got out with the shotgun in his hands.

I followed him and let my gaze stray over the deserted parking lot. At least the store hadn't been hit by bombs. Maybe we'd actually find some food in there. Close to the entrance of the Walmart I noticed one lonely car—an old silver Lincoln.

Dad had parked in the middle of the lot, a fair distance away from the building. Anything out there would be able to see us. The confusion must have showed on my face.

'I want to get an overview of our surroundings, so we don't get ambushed,' Dad said, sounding like an army officer.

Ambushed?

Our steps echoed in the silence as we made our way towards the huge glass doors. My hackles rose. It felt like we were on display. I flashed a glance at

35

the Lincoln, then stopped. Slowly, I turned back and took a closer look at the old car.

'Sherry?'

The Lincoln was clean—it wasn't covered with soot. I looked at the windows of the Walmart, where a thick layer of black filth obstructed the view into the store. So why wasn't the car covered in soot too? It didn't make sense.

'Sherry?' Dad's steps came closer. He stopped beside me and followed my gaze.

'Someone used the car after the...' I swallowed hard. '...after the bombardment.'

Dad looked around, as if he was expecting the owner to be nearby, but everything was silent, except for the cooing of a group of pigeons sitting on the roof of the building. My body began to prickle, as if millions of ants were crawling over my skin.

'Let's look for a way into the store,' Dad said, with a nod at the grimy glass doors.

As we stood before them, I cleaned the soot from a section of glass and peered through. It took my eyes a moment to focus. Shelves were thrown over, and packaging littered most of the floor. The store was a mess.

'Others have been in there,' I said as I stepped back. Hopefully they hadn't taken all the food.

Dad tried to open the doors but they didn't budge. 'Let's go round the back. Maybe there's another entrance.' He led the way and I followed a few steps behind.

On the other side, the doors were destroyed. Shards of razor-sharp glass covered the ground and glittered in the sunlight. Something red caught my eye. I took a closer look. Bloodstains splattered the concrete and some of the shards were smeared with

36

it. I held the pistol a bit tighter. Maybe a stray dog had injured its paws.

Sure.

Chills ran down my back.

Dad didn't acknowledge the blood. Maybe he didn't want to worry me.

Too late.

He was focused on the inside of the building. I took a step forwards, but he raised his arm, palm out.

I stopped and listened.

Silence.

1,141 days I'd longed for silence. But now that I finally had it, I couldn't bear it.

Dad walked slowly into the building. I waited, my foot tapping a nervous rhythm on the concrete. After a moment, he glanced over his shoulder and gave a nod. 'It's okay.'

I jumped over the broken glass, careful not to step on it—the shards would easily slice through my thin sneakers.

The inside of the store was dim, the halogen ceiling lamps useless without power. The only sources of light were the two glass-fronted entrances. Because of the soot covering them and the enormous size of the store, it wasn't nearly enough.

It was impossibly stuffy. The early afternoon heat had warmed the air and the store felt like a sauna. I turned up the long sleeves of my shirt and the legs of my jeans.

'Sherry, come on,' Dad urged. Beads of sweat glistened on his forehead. His T-shirt was drenched and clung to his too-thin body. After the years in the air-conditioned bunker, we weren't used to summer heat.

Slowly we moved further into the store. Shelves had toppled, and torn clothes, destroyed books and shredded packaging littered the ground. Dad headed for the electrical products. What did he want there?

He searched the shelves and the ground, tearing at boxes that lay in the litter. A few minutes later, he'd found a radio and some batteries. He pushed a few buttons and held the mic up to his mouth with a look of elation. I leaned against a shelf of broken laptops as he spoke into the mic, then waited for someone to reply. His smile disappeared as he tried another radio and then another, ripping them out of the boxes. He shook them, as if that would get them working.

The stench of something rotten carried over to us and I scrunched up my nose. Dairy products maybe. Or fruit. The putrid smell hung heavy in the warm air. I breathed through my mouth, but it didn't help.

'Let's find the aisle with cans and cereal,' I said when I could bear it no longer. My stomach was growling like an animal was in there and the thought of cereal, or maybe even candy, made it worse.

1,141 days since I'd had candy, even longer since I'd tasted the smoky sweetness of a s'more. Too long.

Defeated, Dad put the last radio back on its shelf and walked ahead to where the canned food was stored. The shelves were empty, but there were tins all over the floor. My stomach constricted painfully, reminding me how long it was since I had last eaten anything.

I put my pistol in its holster and grabbed a can of sweetcorn. The colours of the label were faded to dull yellow. I flung it to the ground and stomped on it, hoping to break it open, but the only result was a dent. I kicked the can, sending it flying across the aisle. My gaze settled on a pickle jar with a screw top. My stomach did a little somersault. Pickles weren't my favourite, but right then I couldn't have cared less. I picked the jar up and tried to open it.

Glass crunched.

I froze and dropped the pickle jar. It smashed, and bits of glass, pickled vegetables and juice flew everywhere. The sour smell clogged my nose. Pickle juice seeped into my sneakers through a small hole in the sole.

Crunch.

Someone was coming into the store. I scanned my surroundings, my pulse racing, the *thud-thud* of my heart banging in my ears. Dad clasped my arm hard and pulled me behind his back. My foot slipped on a pickle. Dad's fingers dug into my skin, keeping me upright. We listened. I went for the pistol, but my hand shook so much I was worried I'd drop it.

Crunch.

I stared at Dad, my eyes wide. Had they heard us? He put his index finger to his lips. I gave a tiny nod. My breathing felt so loud—could they hear it?

Something rustled in the neighbouring aisle. I backed up, away from the noise. Dad pointed his gun at the shelves that separated our aisle from the other. Maybe it was just a stray dog. Or a wild boar.

More rustling. This time in both neighbouring aisles.

Maybe a group of wild boars.

Or maybe something far worse.

I pressed myself closer to Dad. A low grumble came from the aisle to our left. I bit down on my lower lip to keep myself from making a noise.

A creak. I lifted my head and saw the huge shelf

above us tipping over. Someone...or something... was pushing it—and it would crush us.

Dad's grip tightened and he dragged me after him. We ran down the aisle, stumbling over cans. Our steps echoed through the store, drowning out any other noises. Sweat drenched my body. At the end of the aisle, Dad let go of me. I glanced at him in confusion. He shot in the direction where the grumble had come from. Once. Twice.

A roar rang out in the store, feral and angry. It sounded big. Dangerous. Terrifying.

'Run, Sherry!' he shouted as he shot again. 'Run!'

So I ran. And as I did, I registered movement from the corner of my eye.

I ran faster, back towards the broken entrance of the store. Glass crunched under my sneakers and a sharp pain shot through my right foot. I ignored it and kept running.

Three years of cycling to produce energy had made me fit, but panic corded up my body and my throat felt strangled. The sun blinded me as I rounded the building and crossed the parking lot.

Our car came into view, finally.

I glanced over my shoulder, expecting to see Dad behind me, but he wasn't there. There was no one. Nothing.

I was alone. My steps slowed. I gasped for breath, my eyes searching the parking lot for a sign of Dad. Or something else.

Nothing.

I blinked at the building, my eyes wide. 'Dad?'

Gunshots rang out in the silence.

'*Dad!*' I screamed. Blood hammered through my veins. Before I knew what I was doing, I had run back to the entrance. My arms were outstretched, pistol aimed at the inside of the building. It was silent again.

My breathing was harsh and tears prickled my eyes. I took a hesitant step forward. 'Dad?' I called in a shaky voice.

No answer.

After the sun, it seemed even darker inside than I remembered. My eyes had difficulty making out much. The back of the vast store lay in shadows.

I took another step forward and another, until I stood in the front area of the store. Dad was somewhere in here—he had to be. And he needed my help.

I took a deep breath, then I walked further into the store. My gun hand was still shaking. If Dad hadn't stopped our attackers with his shotgun, how could I possibly do it?

Calm down. Breathe.

I headed for the aisle with the canned food, my steps slow and measured.

I glanced over my shoulder. Had something just moved? I turned and pointed the pistol in that direction.

A rack of cotton nightgowns spun very slowly. There was no wind in the store, so why was it turning?

I wiped sweat from my forehead. Get a grip, Sherry.

I took another breath and moved towards the aisle where Dad and I had heard the noises. The shelf hadn't toppled over, it still stood in place.

I slipped on something. My right leg gave way and I landed with a heavy thud on my backside. Pain shot up my back. I'd dropped the pistol. It lay next to my left foot. I scrambled to my knees and reached

41

for it.

Then I froze.

The gun lay in a little puddle of blood. With shaky fingers, I grabbed it. The blood was still warm.

Oh God.

I took a deep breath. With a little retch, I wiped the bloody pistol on my jeans.

A rustling caught my attention, and I tensed. I couldn't tell where it had come from. Slowly, I straightened up. Something rushed past the end of the aisle. I released the safety catch, my breath coming in little gasps.

'Dad?' My voice quivered.

Clicking, not unlike the sound of Grandma's knitting needles, came from nearby. Clicking—like claws on tiles.

'Dad!' I cried desperately.

The clicking came closer and I stumbled backwards. Something appeared at the end of the aisle. In the dim light, I could just make out a silhouette. It looked like a human, but was hunched over and partly covered with grey hair.

Our eyes met. There was a flicker of yellow there, like a spark of madness. Or raw hunger. I took a step back. A big mistake.

The creature hurled itself towards me.

Never run from a predator, or you turn into their prey. I remembered Grandpa's words a second too late.

I shot twice. The creature roared, and goosebumps flashed across my skin.

Click-click-click-click...

Claws scratching the floor, spit flying, the beast closed in on me. Muscles rippled under its patchy fur.

42

I whirled around. I tried to shoot while I ran, but my bullets hit only shelves.

It was still behind me.

Something bumped against my calves and made me stumble. I fell forward and cushioned the fall with my hands. Pain shot through my arms.

This time I didn't let go of the gun. I shot at the moving shadow and was pushed backwards. The back of my head hit something with a sickening thud. My vision went black for a moment.

I shot blindly until there weren't any bullets left. My gun hand dropped down into my lap. A growling to my right made me shrink back, and I raised the pistol to hit the creature over the head.

Shots in close proximity startled me and my eyes opened wide. My vision was returning slowly. Something warm was trickling down my neck and soaking my shirt. Blood. Maybe I was bleeding to death.

Through the haze, I watched the creature drop to the ground. I scrambled backwards, not wanting to be anywhere near this thing, no matter if it was dead or alive. Bullet wounds littered its hairy body, oozing blood. A milky liquid flowed from its eyes—it looked like it was crying.

Something touched my arm and a scream ripped from my throat.

Stupid locker. Stuck again. I yanked. Nothing.

I yanked harder. It swung open fast and I stumbled back.

Stupid thing.

I pushed my bag into it.

'You dropped something.'

Alex.

I turned so fast, my neck cracked. My skin flushed with heat. He was much closer than I'd expected.

'Did you hear what I said?'

'Huh?' More heat flooded my cheeks.

'You dropped something.' Alex pointed at the ground. A sheet of paper lay on the linoleum, just centimetres from my feet.

I bent down and my head collided with his.

'Ouch.'

God, I was such an idiot.

'I'm sorry.'

I ripped the piece of paper from his hand. With a mumbled thanks, I dashed away.

CHAPTER FOUR

I sat up but the movement made the dizziness worse. My vision was still blurry. A person stood in front of me—for a fleeting moment, I thought it might be Dad, but he was too young and his hair wasn't red. I struggled when he tried to lift me.

'Stop it, or I'll leave you here. More of them will be here soon,' he hissed.

He picked me up and straightened with a small groan. Then he carried me through the store and out of the building to a car.

'My dad…' I tried to get the words out.

'Can you stand?'

I nodded numbly and clung to his T-shirt when he set me down on my feet. He wrapped his arm around my waist to keep me steady and I leaned my head against his chest.

I almost fell into the passenger seat when he opened the door for me. The purr of the engine brought me back to my senses.

'My father's still in the store,' I said groggily.

He shook his head as he steered the car across the parking lot. The speed threw me against the door and I was too weak to keep myself upright.

'No. Nobody's in there. Except for two dead Weepers.'

'But my father—' I began, but he interrupted me.

'Believe me, he isn't in there.'

I took a shaky breath. The heat was getting to me. My head was aching where I'd hit it, and I felt woozy. 'It's stuffy. Can we open the windows?'

He shook his head. 'No. You're bleeding all over

47

the place. They're like sharks. The smell of blood attracts them. They'd follow us and I won't risk that.'

I frowned at him. 'How do you know that they aren't following us already?'

'I just know it,' he replied and returned his gaze to the windshield.

The car was going at a maddening speed. Every bump in the concrete catapulted me off the passenger seat, bringing my head dangerously close to the ceiling. The car was definitely travelling at its limits, and there wasn't any traffic to slow us down.

'This was the car in the parking lot? The Lincoln. Why was your car in the parking lot?' I slurred like a drunk.

'I was hunting. I heard gunshots,' he replied casually.

Hunting? Maybe he'd been after the wild boars.

I breathed deeply, but it didn't help to clear my mind. 'Where are you taking me?' I asked, my eyes half-closed.

'Somewhere safe. Maybe you should close your eyes for a little while. You look like shit.'

I stared at the windshield and listened to the noise of the engine. My hands were coated with blood, still sticky. Dad's blood. My throat tightened. I closed my eyes. Images of him being ripped apart, torn into tiny pieces, flashed into my mind.

Dad.

I'd abandoned him, failed him. My fault. All my fault. I swallowed hard, trying to stop myself from crying.

After a while, when I felt steadier, I tilted my head to the side to look at the profile of the boy beside me. He had high cheekbones and tanned skin. 'My name is Sherry.'

He glanced at me. 'Joshua,' he said with a fleeting smile, before handing me an old towel. 'To stop the bleeding.' He turned back to the road and I pressed the towel against my head.

'What happened to my father?' I asked, though I wasn't sure if I wanted to know.

'I don't know. But since I didn't see a body, I guess they took him with them.'

'Took him with them? Where?'

'I'm not entirely sure. There are a few places where the Weepers live.'

'Weepers?'

'That's what everyone calls the infected.'

I stared at him.

'They look like they're crying. When you're face-to-face with them, you'll know what I mean.'

An image of the dead mutant—Weeper—flashed into my mind.

'But why would they take my father with them?'

He shrugged. 'They stockpile.'

'Stockpile?'

'Like squirrels.'

I clamped a palm over my mouth to stifle a sob. Do. Not. Cry. I swallowed and dropped my hand. 'You mean, they eat humans?'

He nodded, his eyes focused on the street. A shotgun was resting across his lap. 'Yes—easy prey. Humans have forgotten how to survive in a battle of the fittest. Our instincts are dormant, and the Weepers prefer easy prey.' He pulled off the freeway and onto a smaller street.

'But weren't they like us once?' I croaked.

He pulled his gaze from the windshield and smiled sadly. 'But they don't know that. The virus has

49

turned them into predators without a conscience. They've lost their memories of who they were.'

I couldn't stop myself from imagining that creature chewing on Dad. Horror exploded within me.

'We have to save him!' I shouted.

He glanced at me, studying my expression before he shook his head. Desperate, I reached out and tried to grab the steering wheel, but he knocked my hand away. 'Have you lost your mind?'

'What if he's still alive? I can't let…that…happen to him!' Waves of terror for Dad washed over me. And what about Mom? How could I explain it to her? She'd never forgive me. I began to hyperventilate as a new fear struck me. Mom! 'My family—I have to get back to them! They're still in our house, in a bunker. I need to warn them about the Weepers!'

Joshua didn't slow the car. 'We can't go back now. Even if we could save your dad—and I'm not promising anything—it'll be getting dark soon, and the night is the time for predators. Believe me, you don't want to be on the street when they're on the prowl—they'll sniff out your blood before you even see them, and then you won't be able to save yourself, let alone your dad. As for your family, as long as they stay in the bunker, they should be fine.'

I shivered. 'But my father told them to find other people if we haven't returned by tomorrow.'

Joshua's brows dipped in a frown. 'Look, we need to spend the night outside the city. But we can search for your father and go back for your family tomorrow after sunrise.'

I had no choice. 'Okay,' I managed to croak out.

The moment the word left my mouth, guilt pulled at my throat. Joshua touched my shoulder briefly. 'There's nothing more we can do tonight. And your

50

family will be fine. The bunker has kept you safe until now, hasn't it?'

I nodded. 'We've spent the last 1,141 days there.' Surely it would keep them safe another night. Some of the pressure lifted from my chest, allowing me to take a deep breath.

'You counted the days?' He smiled.

'There wasn't much else to do.' I stared at my lap, where my jeans were smeared with blood. Dad's blood. I ran my fingertips over the rough material.

'1,141 days is a long time.'

I glanced at him. He was staring at the road as he spoke.

'I spent 515 days in a bunker.'

I raised my eyebrows. 'You counted the days too?'

One corner of his mouth pulled up in a lopsided grin. 'Yeah.'

'Why did you leave your bunker? Did the military make contact?'

His mouth set in a thin line. 'The military never showed up—they just broadcast their useless warning.' His eyes flickered towards me. 'It was a public bunker. Things escalated pretty fast.'

He turned his face away and stared out of the windshield.

'My father and I left the bunker because we'd run out of food...' I began, but guilt and grief gripped me at the thought of Dad, and I slipped into silence, tension crackling like static in the air.

Joshua's jaw tightened. I stared out of the side window and watched the landscape as it passed us by. Broken-down cars littered the streets, rusty and covered in dirt. Fallen debris lay everywhere. Was Dad out there somewhere, waiting for me to help him?

51

We slowed down and turned onto a narrow dirt track. We were driving away from the coast and into the surrounding hills. I still hadn't seen any other human being except Joshua. He stayed silent during the rest of the drive. I didn't know what to say to him. It had been so long since I'd dealt with other people. Maybe I was out of practice.

I sat up when we neared a huge villa with smaller cottages surrounding the main building. It must have been a winery; the surrounding slopes were overgrown with vines heavy with grapes. The sweet smell of rotten fruit carried into the car, sweeter than anything I'd smelled in a while. We drove through a set of iron gates. A stone wall, overgrown with ivy, surrounded the buildings, reminding me of pictures of France or Tuscany.

We pulled up in front of the main house. The ochre paint was peeling off and a few of the clay shingles were missing. The white of the window shutters had faded to a dull grey, and two of them swayed precariously in the wind.

Joshua got out of the car without a word and slammed the door shut. I glanced at the small clock on the dashboard. The journey had taken us a little over an hour. No traffic, no stop lights, no speed limits. Just us and the Lincoln flying over dead freeways. Los Angeles had turned into a still life.

I got out of the car, but had to grab the door to steady myself. Joshua took my arm. 'Don't fall. Your head's only just stopped bleeding. Come on.'

He led me towards the main building. Every time my right foot touched the ground it burned with agony, and the pebbles covering the courtyard dug into my soles, sending jolts of pain through my feet and up my neck.

'Where are we?'

The sun hung lower in the sky now, so it didn't dazzle me when I looked up at him. He was almost a head taller than me. His skin tone reminded me of the honey Grandma used to make. The buzzing of bees and the taste of home-made honey had once belonged to my summer, like sunshine and ice cream. Not any more.

1,148 days since Grandma had given up her beehive. It had felt like more than a goodbye to her bees.

He shrugged. 'People here call it Safe-haven. A few other survivors live in the winery with me.'

The wooden door of the main building was dark, maybe oak, and it was cross-braced with iron, which gave it a medieval touch. Joshua opened it with an old-fashioned silver key that he'd taken from his jeans pocket. Loss of blood and lack of food were taking their toll on me. All I wanted to do was to lie down, close my eyes and sleep.

It was slightly cooler in the house than outside, but the heat was still bothering me. The hall was dimly lit and a wooden staircase led up to the first floor. A flowery carpet covered the ground and a silver chandelier hung from the ceiling. The owner must have been rich.

'Come on,' Joshua said. He wrapped his arm more tightly around my waist and walked me towards the door on our right. It led into a huge living room with the same flowery carpet. I hoped I wouldn't bleed on it.

That's your main concern? a snarky little voice in my brain asked. I shook my head to get rid of it, but that only worsened my headache. Sweat trickled into my eyes, making them sting. I blinked a few

53

times to clear my vision.

A middle-aged woman sat in an armchair, her head leaning against the backrest and her eyes closed. A book lay open on her lap, and several piles of books and papers littered the floor beside her feet. Her short brown hair was streaked with grey. Crinkles lined the skin around her eyes and mouth. A few more armchairs and a sofa were positioned in front of a huge fireplace. The room was clean, free of dust or soot. It was obvious people lived here.

'Karen, there's someone here who needs your help,' Joshua said, all but dragging me into the room.

Karen's eyes shot open. They were light grey and seemed to pierce right through me. Her gaze swept over my body for a second before she got up so fast it startled me.

'Joshua!' she exclaimed. She held a hand to her cheek, her lips parted in surprise. 'What happened?' She hustled over to us in a few steps. Her smile was reassuring and I tried to smile in return, but I wasn't sure if it worked.

Together they helped me towards the sofa and made me sit down. I slumped against the soft leather of the backrest. Finally, the pain in my foot lessened.

'When I found her, two Weepers had picked her for dinner. They'd have killed her if she hadn't fired off her gun in every direction,' Joshua told Karen with a hint of dark amusement.

I glanced at him. His eyes sparkled and his words had sounded like praise. But what did I know? My social skills had suffered during three years in the bunker.

Karen prodded a tender spot on my head, making me wince and stopping my train of thought.

She clucked her tongue in disapproval. 'Lots of blood. Nasty gash. That needs stitches.'

I groaned and Joshua chuckled, earning himself a glare from me. Judging by the widening of his smile, that seemed to amuse him even more. He really had nice teeth, straight and white. I ran my tongue over my own teeth.

'Karen knows what she's doing, don't worry.' He winked.

Karen walked out of the room and returned with a small bag. She pulled out a needle, bandages and some thread, and placed the items on the small side table next to the sofa. It made me think of a surgeon's theatre. Equipment in hand, she moved around the sofa and stopped behind me. 'Lean forward.'

I did so without hesitation. That way, at least I wouldn't see the needle. The movement made my temples throb and black dots danced in my vision.

'Razor.' She held a hand out and Joshua put a small razor on her palm.

I tilted my head, frowning at him. 'Razor?'

'She needs to remove the hair around the wound, so she can stitch you up.'

'As long as I don't end up with a bald head.' I'd never been too fond of my reddish-blonde hair, but I definitely preferred it to no hair at all.

'Maybe it would suit you.' Joshua smirked.

As I looked down again, the throbbing in my temples turned into a full-blown hammering, as if someone was trying to split my skull. My vision darkened and I sagged forward. Joshua moved over and wrapped an arm around my shoulders to keep me in a sitting position. His grip was strong, his body warm. He smelled of pine needles and fresh laundry. I wanted to breathe in the smell and close my eyes.

Maybe it would alleviate the pain in my head.

'I'll only shave the hair around the wound. It won't be visible.' Karen patted my shoulder gently while she pushed my hair away, and I could feel the blade go to work on my skin.

'Now I'll do the stitches.'

My shoulders stiffened. This wouldn't be pleasant. Joshua held my hand. It was tan and strong, his nails cut very short. It gave me a sense of safety, like nothing could happen to me as long as Joshua was around. I sighed. A second later, he straightened up. 'I'll look for Geoffrey. I'm sure he'd want to know that there's a new arrival. He'll be ecstatic.'

I watched him leave the room, quelling the feeling of panic in my stomach. Without him, I felt vulnerable.

I tried not to wince when the needle pierced my skin. 'Ouch.'

Karen pushed my head down. 'You'll get used to it. In the beginning Joshua always flinched when I stitched him up, but after a few dozen wounds it becomes routine.'

A few dozen wounds? I stared at the flowery design of the carpet. 'Why does he need stitches all the time?'

Karen let out a sigh and paused briefly with the needle, giving me a moment to breathe deeply.

'The hunt is dangerous. I'm always relieved when he comes back with just a gash or a bruise. I worry that some day he won't come back at all. Anyway, he won't listen. He's too stubborn.'

I opened my mouth to ask her about the hunt, but she kept talking.

'You know, I was a nurse in my other life.'

'Your other life?' I echoed.

'That's what we call the time before the rabies.

56

Better times.' She paused. When she continued, it was almost as if she was speaking to herself. 'Isn't it strange how we still call it "rabies", even though this virus is so much more deadly? I treated people with the "old" rabies in my other life and *they* didn't try to eat me.'

I gave a nod, not quite taking in her words, then flinched as she began stitching again.

'You need to keep still.' She paused. 'Joshua didn't even tell me your name.'

'Sherry,' I said quietly. Tears prickled in my eyes from the pain in my head, and from frightening thoughts of Dad. They were never far from my mind, no matter how hard I tried to force them away.

'It's nice to see a new face. It gives me hope.' Her voice broke slightly at the end. She cleared her throat. 'Like I said, I was a nurse. Thanks to Joshua, I don't get out of practice. My husband was a teacher.'

'Is he…?' I trailed off, uncertain how to end the question.

'He's alive. He lives here with me.'

I was happy for her. I'd seen what losing a loved one did to people. Grandma had never been the same since Grandpa died.

'How long have you been in Safe-haven?'

Karen pursed her lips in thought. 'A little over a year.'

'Over a year?' How had they survived the Weepers? Dad and I hadn't even managed to last more than a few hours on our own.

'It isn't easy, but we stick together,' Karen said.

It was comforting to know that they'd survived in this new world for so long. Maybe there was a chance for my family.

'How many people live here?' I managed not to move my head now as I spoke. I was a fast learner—though my homeroom teacher might have disputed that.

'There's Joshua, my husband Larry, Geoffrey, Marie and her daughter Emma, and Tyler, though we don't know if that's his actual name—we call him Tyler because the name's tattooed on his wrist.' She dropped my hair and clapped her hands. 'Done.'

'Why don't you know if it's his real name?'

Karen walked around the sofa and sat on the armrest next to me. 'Tyler doesn't speak. I don't think he remembers much. When Joshua found him, he was in a very bad way.' She swallowed hard and looked out of the window. The sun was setting beyond the hills.

'Do you have other wounds I need to tend to?' Her eyes searched over me.

I nodded. 'I've got a few bruises, but they'll probably heal. My right foot hurts though. I stepped on broken glass when I ran away.'

Guilt burned through me. If I hadn't run away, would Dad be with me now?

Karen got down on her knees. Carefully, she slipped off my sneaker and blood-sticky sock. I winced as she pulled away the sodden cotton. She inspected the sole of my foot with a deep frown. 'More stitches,' she said with an apologetic smile. I took a deep breath through my nose and leaned my head against the backrest, my eyes squeezed shut.

Karen was careful and fast, but the stitches still hurt like hell. Much worse than the stitches in the back of my head.

'Are you the only survivors? Has the military

contacted you?' I was scared of the answer.

Karen shook her head. She bandaged my foot and then lowered it gently to the ground. I relaxed.

'No, the military only sent their warnings, but we've had contact with two other safe havens in California. Sadly, our radio receiver didn't allow long-distance broadcasting, so we don't know about survivors in the rest of the country. And now that our radio has stopped working, we can't communicate at all.'

There were other survivors. I felt my shoulders relax. 'Do you know if the rabies has spread beyond North America? Is there any way for us to contact the military?'

She looked at me. 'Oh, Sherry. There isn't any military left. The rabies destroyed everything.'

Someone was shouting outside. I glanced up from my homework. More shouts. A fight. One of the voices was Bobby. What was he doing outside so close to curfew? We'd get into trouble because of him. I walked towards the window and looked out. Bobby stood on the sidewalk, surrounded by older boys. Pushing him. Laughing at him.

The tallest boy pushed Bobby's shoulder. He lost his balance, fell to the ground. His eyes were wide, his lips trembling.

My steps resounded on the asphalt. The boys looked up. Smirks. They thought they were cool. Idiots.

'Leave him alone,' I told them.

Snickers. 'The little boy needs a girl to protect him. Is she your girlfriend?'

What a dumb-ass.

Bobby's face turned red, his eyes moist.

'I'm his sister. Now get lost.'

I pushed into their circle and stood in front of Bobby. The boys were older than me. Taller. Stupid wannabe machos. Trying to intimidate me.

'Get lost, bitch.'

I froze. My fingers curled, forming a fist.

I really liked the way my knuckles collided with his chin.

CHAPTER FIVE

A short, thin man with shoulder-length hair stood in the doorway, smiling at me. When our eyes met, his smile widened to reveal yellowish teeth. A front tooth was missing. Streaks of grey in his black hair, and his wrinkled, worn-out clothes added to his messy look. I couldn't help but smile back.

Joshua appeared in the background, towering over the man. He squeezed past him into the living room and sank down in an armchair. 'That's Geoffrey.' He nodded towards the door.

Geoffrey shook his head as if Joshua had committed a serious crime. 'That isn't a proper introduction,' he said as he walked towards me. Holding out his hand, he bowed his head. 'Geoffrey Hall. Back in my day, men were taught proper conduct towards women.'

Joshua's face darkened in a scowl. 'Those times are over. No one cares about manners any more. They're too busy surviving.' He swung his legs over the armrest, as if to prove a point.

Geoffrey let go of my hand as if scolded, nodding his head like a reprimanded child. 'Yes, yes. They're over, aren't they?'

Karen frowned at Joshua before she walked out of the room, muttering under her breath. It was obvious that she found his comment unnecessary. I had to agree with her.

Geoffrey lowered himself into the armchair next to Joshua and took a piece of paper from the pocket of his khakis. He unfolded it, then put it on the table. His expression grew wistful as he smoothed the paper out almost lovingly. I glanced at Joshua for an explanation, but he was busy staring out the window.

'That's how I looked in my other life,' Geoffrey said in a quiet voice.

I moved to the edge of the sofa to get a better look. It was a cutting from a science magazine. The paper was yellow, its edges ragged. I rested my elbows on the table and stared at it. The man in the picture was Geoffrey. And yet he wasn't. The man in the photo was accepting a science award. He was wearing a black suit, his short, black hair slicked back. He looked proud, smug even. The Geoffrey in front of me was nothing but a shadow of that man.

'It started out innocently. When we began researching rabies, it was just out of scientific curiosity.' He looked up at me and smiled apologetically. I tried to follow his words. 'Curiosity's a good thing, isn't it? It brought technology to mankind, it's essential for progress.'

I wasn't sure why he was telling me this, what he wanted me to say. But I began to feel uneasy. 'You were researching rabies?'

Geoffrey stared down at his folded hands. 'I explored the possibilities of the virus, its limits and usefulness.'

This new explanation seemed more confusing than the one before.

'I don't get it. Useful for what?'

'You have to understand, I didn't personally create the last version of the virus. But I was involved in the beginnings of the research, like so many others. None of us knew that the military planned to use the altered virus as a biological weapon. If I'd known...' He closed his eyes and shook his head.

I forced a neutral expression, though I felt sick.

I couldn't believe what I'd just heard.

I'd always thought that the mutated rabies was just a freak twist of nature—that's what the government had said. But it wasn't. It wasn't just bad luck, fate or God's punishment. It was man-made. The realization made me dizzy for a moment. The government had lied to us about the mutation. What else had they kept from us?

And Geoffrey?

This man was responsible for the death of millions, likely billions of people. My friends were dead, my hometown destroyed. All because of a few scientists who wanted to play God? I glanced at Joshua, wondering what he was thinking. He stayed silent, but watched me with an unreadable expression.

'We thought we could handle the virus. We thought it could be destroyed. But we couldn't stop it. Nobody could. We were powerless.' Geoffrey opened his eyes to stare at me. They were filled with horror. 'Absolutely powerless.' His voice had become so quiet that I had to move closer to hear him.

I swallowed, trying to ignore the pounding in my temples. 'What happened to Los Angeles? It looks like it's been bombed.'

Geoffrey smiled, but something in his eyes changed. 'The rabies virus was particularly nasty on the west coast. The infected were prowling the street—more and more every day. People in parts of the country that hadn't been affected began to panic.' He paused and looked up at me like a beaten dog. 'They screamed for the government to do something, but the government hesitated. It was only when the virus had gotten totally out of control that they chose to bombard Los Angeles and San

65

Francisco. Their inhabitants were already in bunkers, so they couldn't protest. The military and the government were certain that it was the only way to stop the madness. It didn't work, though.'

'Why didn't they broadcast a warning?'

He smiled sheepishly. 'We didn't know much about the virus and the mutation. The military was worried that the infected might be listening in. They thought they'd run for safety before they could be destroyed.'

'The Weepers behave like beasts, but they are intelligent. *Very* intelligent, and that makes them dangerous,' Joshua explained. He rested his head against the back of the armchair while he gazed at the ceiling.

'But if so many people died, where are their bodies? There must have been thousands of them.'

Geoffrey stared intently at the paper as he spoke. 'They were burned. The military feared an epidemic. They put the bodies in a pile and burned them. The crematoriums were swamped and most of them were closed anyway. The smell of burned flesh hung over the city for days.' He closed his eyes tightly. It took him a few minutes to compose himself.

I swallowed down my nausea. 'But there must be members of the government somewhere, or military,' I said.

Geoffrey shrugged and looked away. 'I've no idea. I've told you everything I know.'

His voice changed suddenly, as if he had unburdened himself. 'Joshua told me that the Weepers captured your father. I hope you manage to get to him in time.' He patted my shoulder awkwardly before he rose from the armchair and excused himself.

I watched his back as he walked out—not sure if I should hate him, or feel sorry for him. My fingers traced the bloodstains on my jeans. Dad's blood. He was all alone, probably unable to defend himself. Was he waiting for me to save him? Did he think I'd abandoned him? My stomach twisted with worry and guilt. I felt like I was going to throw up. This was all too much. When I finally looked up, Joshua was leaning forward, watching me with curiosity.

I rubbed my temples. 'Does Geoffrey tell his story to every newcomer?'

'Pretty much.'

'I'd have thought that's something he'd want to keep to himself.' By God, if I'd screwed up like that, if I'd killed so many people, I'd keep my mouth shut.

'I guess he wants to get it out of his system. Seems to weigh heavy on him. I mean it's some really tough shit. He'd be a heartless bastard if it didn't bother him.'

'Do you believe him?'

Joshua hesitated. 'I haven't found anything that would prove him wrong. Why would he lie?'

Yes, why?

'Don't you blame him for everything?'

For a moment, Joshua didn't react. He stared up at the ceiling again, as if there lay the answer to all our problems. I'd almost given up on getting a reply when he spoke in a very quiet voice. 'When he first told me what he just told you…yes, I hated him. Hated him for all I'd lost, for all I'd seen.' He closed his eyes and clenched his jaw, the muscles twitching beneath his tanned skin. 'But then I realized that he'd lost just as much as the rest of us. More, even. And he's tried to make up for his failure—unlike many others.' Joshua opened his eyes and turned to

67

look at me, a vein pulsing in his forehead. I raised my eyebrows, willing him to explain.

'His wife and children died from the rabies. He watched it happen. There was nothing he could do. Once people are infected, all you can do is watch them die or watch them turn.'

I wrapped my arms around myself. 'That's horrible.'

Joshua gave a small nod. 'Geoffrey never went into shelter. He tried to help the military stop the spread. I met him a few months after I'd left the bunker.' The slightest hint of admiration lay in his tone.

'But why did so many people die? And why have some survived?'

Joshua ran a hand through his hair. 'Geoffrey told me that about ten per cent of the population are immune to the rabies, maybe even less. When people began leaving the bunkers, the virus was still highly contagious and the majority got infected. Almost all of them died. Those that didn't die are now howling in the streets.'

'But if ten per cent are immune, why are there so few left?'

Joshua stared at the ground, clenching his hands into fists. 'After a few months, the mood in the public bunkers became...irritable. People lost it over nothing. There were fights and shootings. That's why people in public bunkers went outside much sooner than your family. And outside they were easy prey.'

The room no longer seemed warm. 'How do I know if I'm immune?'

'Geoffrey says it isn't contagious any more—only if you get the bodily fluids of a Weeper or infected

68

person in your bloodstream...or something like that.' He shrugged one shoulder. 'I guess I'm immune.'

'So my father might not get the virus?' I asked in a whisper. *If he's still alive, if the Weepers haven't eaten him.* My fingernails dug into my palms.

Joshua dropped his legs from the armrest and stood. 'If he's not bitten.'

He walked towards a cupboard and took a few boxes of bullets and several weapons from it. Five were smaller guns, one was a shotgun. He came back to the sofa and sank down beside me. After he'd put the weapons on the table, he began loading them.

'We'll set out tomorrow, just after sunrise. Then we should have enough time to get your family and bring them back here. After that, we'll look for your father. The chances are slim that he's still alive, but we'll try.'

The chances are slim. The words repeated themselves in my head.

'Maybe it would be better if we began with the search for my dad.'

Joshua shook his head. 'It might take hours or days to locate your father. We don't even know if he's still alive. We should first save those who have the best chance of survival, and that's the rest of your family.'

That made sense. I gulped and gave a small nod. 'How...how long do the Weepers keep their...prey?'

The question felt wrong. Humans weren't prey. An image of Dad in some dark basement waiting to be used as food wouldn't leave my mind.

He shrugged. 'I'm not sure. This isn't something you watch on the Discovery Channel, or read in a

69

science book. I guess they keep some of them for days or even weeks. Maybe they even stockpile for winter, but it's too early for that.' His voice was emotionless, calm even. It made me furious.

'How can you be so relaxed about all this? Don't you care at all?' My hands clenched into fists.

He pulled his gaze up and looked me square in the eyes. 'I do care. That's why I hunt them. But if you've seen what I have, then you learn to deal with the murders and disappearances. You learn to push it aside and move on. The other life isn't here any more. This new world has its own rules. Survival of the fittest is one of them. If you're hoping for kindness and pity, don't hold your breath. I left the shelter with two dozen other people. Now, I'm the only survivor.'

So much death. The thought made me ill. 'I'm sorry. I don't know how you do it,' I admitted in a whisper.

A sad smile broke on his face. 'You get used to it. You need to. It's not a choice, it's a necessity.'

My stomach disrupted the silence with a growl.

'Come on. We'll get you something to eat,' Joshua said, and got up from the sofa. 'I should've thought about that.'

I followed him out of the living room, trying to keep the weight off my injured foot. Joshua noticed and wrapped an arm around my waist. He picked me up, pressing my body against his chest. I let out an embarrassing squeak. I leaned my head against his shoulder, wondering if he could feel the heat of my cheeks through his shirt. I could feel *his* warmth. His skin smelled of the forest, and I had to stop myself from burying my nose in his neck. It felt strange to be this close to someone who wasn't a member of my family.

He carried me through the hall and into a huge kitchen. At its centre was a long, wooden table that could have seated at least eight people. Joshua put me down on my feet and let go of my waist. My skin tingled where it had been pressed against him.

I spotted apples in a bowl and froze. It had been years since I'd had an apple. I tried to remember how it tasted. Joshua followed my gaze and a grin spread across his face. He grabbed an apple and threw it in my direction. I caught it in my outstretched hands. One side was yellow-green, the other a deep red. Reverently, I brought it to my mouth. Mmm, the scent. Like summer and freedom and happiness.

The first bite tasted like heaven. Juicy and sweet. So good. The second bite was even better. I shut my eyes. The taste of apple—another thing to add to the list of things I'd missed over the last 1,141 days.

1,123 days since I'd had an apple—until now.

'There are apple trees growing in the garden behind the house. Karen and Larry gather them and store them in the basement, or make sauce.'

I smiled in embarrassment, because I'd eaten the apple like a savage. Only the stem had survived my hunger.

Joshua opened the fridge and smirked at me over his shoulder. 'Apples aren't the only things that grow in the garden.' He turned around, his arms full of tomatoes and red peppers. My stomach growled and we both laughed. This small flicker of normality, of happiness, felt so damn good. Joshua fetched a packet of spaghetti from one of the cupboards.

'Where do you get the pasta?'

He filled a pot with water and put it on the stove. 'On my hunts I search houses and stores. Sometimes

71

I find something. In the beginning it was easier. Now there's less food, but at least we've got running water.'

'Didn't you have it before?' I asked.

'The water pipes were broken. Geoffrey and Larry built a water pump and connected it to some of the intact pipes. Most of the time it works.'

While the pasta cooked, we made a sauce with the tomatoes and peppers, then settled at the table. Joshua was a decent cook.

475 days since I'd had pasta—spaghetti with some convenience meatball sauce. Better than what came the following 474 days. Stale oatmeal, beans every way, meat out of a can. Nothing I ever wanted to eat again. Nothing in comparison to this—not even close. This was like Grandma's cooking, like my other life on a fork. Fresh and spicy and alive. The pleasant sourness of tomatoes, the heat of cayenne, the light sweetness of the red peppers, with a big slick of peppery green olive oil.

That was food. I emptied my plate in mere minutes, not caring if I looked like an animal. Afterwards, I leaned back, sated and relaxed. Footsteps on the floor above reminded me of the other inhabitants of Safe-haven. I hadn't even thought of them. Maybe they were hungry.

'Where are the others? Shouldn't we have asked them to eat with us?'

Joshua shook his head before he swallowed his last bite of pasta. 'No, they don't eat this late. Marie and Emma will be in their room. And Larry's probably trying to get the radio receiver working again.'

'And Tyler?' I asked.

His expression brightened. 'Karen told you about

72

everyone, didn't she?'

'Well, she mentioned names, not much more,' I replied with a small shrug.

'Tyler's likely somewhere in the vineyard, stargazing or something like that. He likes to stroll around. Some of us don't sleep well.' He trailed off. A few strands of his blond hair fell over his eyes.

'And you? Do you sleep well?' I blurted before I could stop myself.

He didn't lift his head but he glanced up briefly. The look in his eyes sent shivers down my back. 'No. If possible I try not to sleep at all.'

'Why?'

I could have slapped myself. He stood abruptly from his chair, almost causing it to topple over. He gathered our plates, carried them over to the sink and washed them hastily, before drying them off. I sat unmoving on my chair and watched him. I bit my lower lip, wishing I'd just kept my mouth shut.

'It's late and we need to set out early. I'll show you to one of the free rooms,' he said as he walked out of the kitchen. To my surprise, he waited for me in the hall and supported me with an arm around the shoulder, but he didn't try to carry me. The touch felt distant—guarded. As if my words had built a wall between us.

We walked awkwardly up the stairs together and he opened a door to our right. Quiet conversation carried over to us from one of the other rooms, but I couldn't make out what they were saying. A man and a woman were talking. Karen and her husband?

'That's your room.' He stepped aside so I could enter.

I took a few hesitant steps into the room before I turned to him. He was already closing the door.

'I'm sorry for being curious. It just slipped out and it's been a while since I've talked to anyone apart from my family.' The words bubbled out of my mouth in a rush. I sounded like an idiot.

Joshua shook his head without looking at me. 'I just don't like to talk about it.' He looked to the floor. 'Maybe I'll tell you about it one day.'

'Okay.' I shifted from one foot to the other. *God, I must look awkward.*

He ran his hand through his hair. 'Goodnight then.' He turned around.

'Um, Joshua?'

He glanced over his shoulder with a barely disguised grin. 'Hmm?'

'I was just wondering where your room is.'

Joshua's eyebrows shot up. He probably thought I was a stalker.

'Just in case anything happens, you know. I'm not used to being alone at night. In the bunker there was always someone around.' And Weepers couldn't get in there. I shut my mouth and felt my face heat even more.

He'd given up hiding his smile. 'It's across the corridor. Wake me if you need help.'

I don't think I managed to hide my relief. 'Thanks.' There were so many things I wanted to thank him for. For saving me, for saying he'd look for my dad, for being there for me.

I think he saw it all in my eyes.

He gave a small nod. 'Get some sleep.'

The door fell shut.

Silence. The darkness seemed to creep through the windows and right into me. I felt so cold. Inside and out. My hands began to shake; light vibrations starting in my fingertips and spreading through my body like ice. An owl hooted outside. A sound like a lament.

Four hours had passed since I'd seen Dad. Six hours since I'd said goodbye to Mom, Bobby, Mia and Grandma. They were hungry. Worried. Scared.

And I had eaten pasta and talked with Joshua. I dragged myself over to the bed and sank down. Tears sprang to my eyes. They trickled over my cheeks and lips, covering the sweet taste of tomatoes and peppers with their bitter saltiness. Selfish and despicable—that's what I was. I sniffed, trying to get a grip. I'd seldom cried in the three years in the bunker. I wouldn't start now.

Enough. Be strong.

I looked down at myself—covered in blood and dirt. My stomach churned at the sight of it. The worst thing: the blood on the jeans wasn't my own. It was Dad's. How badly had the Weepers hurt him? There had been so much blood on the floor in the store.

This had to go. Immediately. Shower. I needed a shower. I opened the door and peeked out. The hall was deserted. But where was the bathroom? I should have asked Joshua.

A howl rang out in the distance.

It wasn't an owl this time. I froze, my heart beginning to pound frantically in my chest.

Another howl.

Closer this time.

They were close by.

Steps made me jump. A scream stuck in my throat as I spun around to face my attacker. My widened eyes focused on Karen, who was coming up the stairs. She smiled when she saw me, but then she noticed the look on my face.

'What's wrong?'

I let out a shaky breath. 'I heard a howl.'

Karen's brows dipped down in worry. Another howl carried over to us. I couldn't tell if it was closer than before. Relief registered on her face. 'Don't worry. Coyotes, they're harmless.'

'Not Weepers?' I hated how my voice shook.

'No, they don't come near Safe-haven. They prefer the cities. You're okay.' She patted my arm gently. 'Were you looking for something?'

My pulse slowed. 'Yes, I need to clean myself and my clothes.' I gestured to the blood and dirt covering me.

Her gaze swept over me. 'Yes. I guess you're right. The bathroom is the last door on the left. You can take a shower if you like. There's enough water.' She considered my clothes with a shake of her head. 'I don't think your clothes can be saved and Joshua won't let you go with him tomorrow smelling of blood. I'll ask Marie if she's got something for you. I think she's your size.'

'Thank you.'

She waved a dismissive hand at me. 'No need to thank me, Sherry. We need to stick together. Now go take a shower.'

The room was small, with only a shower, washbasin and toilet. At least it didn't have mint-green tiles like the bathroom in our bunker. I locked the door and undressed hastily. The water was hot, almost scalding, and I washed the blood from my body. It tinged the water rusty red with swirls and streaks. Red on white—like art. The scent of the shower gel made my mouth water—vanilla and peach. Better than soap, or nothing at all.

426 days since I'd washed my hair with shampoo.

It felt so damn good. I dried myself off and wrapped a towel around myself. Though I'd tried to keep my injured foot away from the water, the bandage was sodden. It stuck to my skin, the shower gel stinging in my wounds.

A knock made me jump.

I tiptoed towards the door and opened it a crack. A young woman with short blonde hair, the length of matchsticks at most, stood in front of me. She smiled tentatively and held a pile of folded clothes out.

'Thanks,' I mumbled with a shy smile.

'I'm Marie,' she introduced herself. 'You're younger than I expected.'

'I'm Sherry.' I bit my lip. 'I'm fifteen.'

Her eyes grew round. 'I didn't mean to offend you.' At least I wasn't the only one who blushed.

I shook my head hastily. 'No, you didn't. You're younger than I thought too. Karen mentioned that you've got a daughter...'

She laughed. 'I'm twenty-two. My daughter turned two a few weeks ago.'

Her daughter had been born in a bunker? Apparently, I didn't hide my surprise very well.

'I got pregnant when I was in the shelter.' Her voice was quiet. Barely a whisper.

Finally she cleared her throat and gave me a weak smile. 'I don't want to keep you awake. From what I've heard, you need your sleep for tomorrow. Good luck.'

I closed the door silently, then slipped into the underwear and black T-shirt she'd given me. The towel wrapped around my waist, I hurried back to my room.

More howls disrupted the silence. Only coyotes.

They were probably looking for food around Safe-haven. Maybe garbage. I was safe for now. Not for long, though.

Shivers crawled over my back when I thought of tomorrow. We'd collect my family from the bunker. We'd find Dad and save him from the Weepers. Then everything would be okay. I shut my eyes, but images of snarling faces with teary eyes and shredded skin kept flashing in my mind.

'You're worse than Nanna, and she's eighty. Hurry up, or the beach will be crowded,' Izzy urged.

Yeah, right, we wouldn't lose a spot just because of a few minutes. Lately, the presence of the military had scared away most beach-goers.

I unlocked the front door and rushed up the stairs. On the last step I froze. There were noises. Moans.

Mom and Dad.

'Eww!'

The noises stopped and footsteps rang out. Shit! Dad stepped into the hall, his belt open and hair dishevelled.

Please let the ground swallow me. I waited.

'Oh, Sherry, it's you…'

'I just forgot my sunglasses.' I looked anywhere but at his face.

'Sure, sure. Get them.' Dad shifted on his feet, still holding his trousers up, his ears and neck beet-red.

Beyond awkward.

At least he wasn't naked. That would have been the icing on the mortification cake.

'Uhh…I'll just get them and then I'm gone. I won't be back until later, so…umm. Bye.'

I've never run the distance to my room and back out of the front door so fast.

CHAPTER SIX

Thoughts of finding Dad's mangled body had kept me awake most of the night, but when I did sleep, nightmares of hunched shadows and weeping monsters had haunted me. Just after I'd drifted off for the last time, a knock jerked me awake. I sat up and rubbed my eyes. Another knock. Louder this time.

'It's almost morning. Get up!' Joshua's shout must have woken the entire house.

'I'm awake!' I shouted back. I scrambled out of bed and winced when my right foot touched the floor. It wasn't as bad as yesterday, but it still hurt. Maybe Karen had painkillers. I slipped into Marie's jeans. Running my fingers through my hair for want of a brush, I walked to the door and opened it. Joshua wasn't there.

I checked the corridor—empty. He'd probably lost patience and gone downstairs. Well, it wasn't like I needed a babysitter. Pushing thoughts of him out of my head, I hurried into the bathroom. My reflection made me grimace. My hair was a matted mess and there were grey bags under my eyes. I looked like the living dead.

1,142 days since I'd stopped caring about such things. I wouldn't start again now.

I rinsed my mouth with water—I didn't want to use someone else's toothbrush—and made my way downstairs, following the voices coming from the kitchen.

Joshua, Geoffrey, Karen and a middle-aged man with glasses and a bald head sat at the table.

81

'Good morning, Sherry.' Karen smiled warmly. 'This is my husband Larry.' She nodded towards the middle-aged man. He gave a small nod. He seemed cautious—not surprising. He didn't know much about me. I guess this new world required a certain amount of wariness.

I shifted nervously on my feet and pulled my hands out of my pockets, not sure if I should join them or stay where I was. Joshua patted the chair next to him. With a grateful smile, I walked over. The smell of warm bread filled the room. Mouthwatering.

I looked longingly at the basket of biscuits in the middle of the table. Karen laughed and pushed the basket over to me. 'Larry baked them this morning. He and Marie are the cooks of our little patchwork family. Enjoy the biscuits. It was our last packet of flour.'

I picked one of the warm biscuits and broke it in half. Steam rose up from its soft insides. I took a bite.

'They're good,' I said between mouthfuls of my second biscuit. The guarded look on Larry's face morphed into an embarrassed smile.

A guy entered the kitchen. He was tall and lanky. His black trousers hung loosely on his hips and his sleeveless shirt revealed tattooed arms and shoulders.

I stopped chewing. With a short nod towards me, he took the chair beside Larry.

'Morning, Tyler. Hungry?' Karen shoved the basket towards him. He picked a biscuit without a word. His head was shaved and his brown eyes were dull. He wasn't much older than Joshua, maybe in his early twenties. Joshua cleared his throat. I tore my gaze from Tyler, my face growing hot. I'd gawked at him like he was an animal in a zoo. How embarrassing.

'I didn't see you come back last night. How long did you stay in the vineyard?' Joshua asked.

Tyler put a pad on the table in front of him and started scribbling. He pushed the pad over to Joshua. I glanced at the words. It was neat handwriting, so I could read the letters easily.

Midnight. Watched the stars.

Joshua sighed. 'You shouldn't be outside alone at night.'

Tyler leaned over and wrote another reply.

Don't worry. Can take care of myself.

'I know you can.'

A grin flitted across Tyler's face as he leaned back and ate the rest of his biscuit.

'Geoffrey suggested that he could drive to your family's home,' Joshua said.

It took a moment before I realized what he'd said. I glanced between him and Geoffrey, swallowed the last bite of biscuit and licked my lips. 'I'm not sure if my mother would trust someone she doesn't know. Dad told her to be careful. She probably wouldn't even open the door of the bunker, or she'd try to shoot you before you got the chance to explain.'

Geoffrey didn't look as if the prospect of getting shot scared him—losing your wife and children likely did that to you.

'Maybe Geoffrey can follow us in his car. Then you can tell your family what they need to know, Geoffrey can bring them here and we can start searching for your dad straight away,' Joshua said, picking a biscuit and munching on it.

'Okay.' I nodded. Then my eyes found the cuckoo clock. It was almost six.

15 hours and about 37 minutes since the Weepers had captured Dad.

About 56,220 seconds.

56,222 seconds.

Too long.

Joshua's eyes searched my face. 'You look pale.'

'I'm fine.' A feeble attempt at lying. I couldn't have sounded more distressed if I'd tried, but Joshua didn't ask further questions. He left the kitchen and returned with a huge backpack.

'We should set out now.'

Electricity shot through me. I didn't need to be told twice. I turned to Karen. 'Can you give me something for my foot? Some painkillers?'

She nodded. 'Of course. Wait a sec.' She walked towards a cupboard, opened the top drawer, and started rummaging. A minute later, she held two small white pills out to me. 'They'll help,' she promised.

I swallowed them with a sip of water. Their bitter taste spread on my tongue. Hopefully they'd take effect soon.

'You sure you want to do this?' Joshua asked.

'Of course. I've got to find my father.'

Joshua studied my face for a moment, and seemed satisfied with what he saw. 'Okay then.' He headed for the corridor, backpack in hand.

Karen wrapped her arms around me in a tight hug. 'Good luck.' She let go and stepped back with a strained smile. Then she put a few biscuits and apples into a bag, before handing it to me. 'Provisions, in case your search takes longer than expected.'

With a last grateful look, I walked out of the kitchen. Larry followed me outside, while Karen hung back to discuss something with Geoffrey.

Larry limped badly. His right leg looked stiff. Probably thanks to the Weepers. A shiver ran down my back when I thought about it. He put a hand on my shoulder.

'Joshua has fought those beasts before. He'll make sure you all come back in one piece.'

I gave him a faint smile, hoping he was right. Geoffrey walked past us towards an old Ford that was parked behind the Lincoln. Joshua had already gotten into his car, so, with a deep breath, I went and took my seat beside him.

When I reached for the seat belt, Joshua stopped my hand.

'Don't. You might need to leave the car fast. The belt will only slow you down.' He turned the key in the ignition, starting the engine. I hoped I wouldn't have to find out how fast I could leave the car.

As we pulled out of the courtyard, Larry and Karen waved us goodbye. Their faces were solemn and pale. It was an expression I'd seen on Grandma's face moments before Grandpa's last breath. Maybe they thought we wouldn't be coming back. I didn't allow myself to consider that possibility.

My hands were sweaty and it was difficult to sit still. Joshua glanced at me a few times. I tried not to fidget, but it was hopeless. Eventually I slumped against the seat and sighed.

'You must stay calm. It's important that you're able to think straight.'

I pursed my lips. 'It's not that easy. What if we're too late? What if he's already…dead?' It took me a moment to get the word out. A burning started behind my eyeballs, but I blinked it away. Mental strength is what sets survivors apart from victims—that's what Grandpa and Dad used to say.

85

Joshua looked at me for a second before he returned his attention to the street. 'We'll get to him in time.' His tone lacked conviction—or maybe I just imagined that.

'Where did you learn to drive? Who taught you?' It was a feeble attempt at trying to distract myself.

'Nobody. I taught myself. I guess my incentive to learn was pretty strong. It was either that, or fall prey to the Weepers because I wasn't fast enough.'

He was talking about it so casually. It was hard to believe that I could ever handle such horror like he did. Maybe I'd think differently in a few months—if I was still alive. Bad thought.

'I can teach you, if you want,' Joshua said.

'Teach me?'

'Driving. I can teach you how to drive.' He patted the steering wheel.

'That would be great.' If we ever got back to Safe-haven. If we survived.

We were silent for the rest of the ride. I gnawed at the patches of chapped skin on my lips, and when we finally reached my neighbourhood, I tasted blood. I peeked out of the windows, trying to spot if anything had changed since yesterday. It hadn't. The street was just as deserted and spooky as before. I let my eyes wander over the grey sky.

A black dot in the distance made me stop. I tried to make out what it was. A bird? It seemed too big and too fast for even an eagle. What was it? But within a few seconds, it had disappeared. And at that moment we passed number forty-five—where Dad and I had seen the bodies of our neighbours.

They were still there. If you didn't look too closely, they appeared to be asleep. A raven dived towards them and landed on the man's chest. It started pecking his face. I swallowed down bile and turned away.

'There.' I pointed at my house. Joshua slowed down and stopped the car in the middle of the street.

'Don't you want to park at the kerb?' I asked.

Joshua lifted a single eyebrow. 'Why? Are you expecting someone to drive along this street anytime soon?'

He had a point.

Geoffrey pulled up behind us and got out of his car, scanning the neighbourhood, his shoulders tense. 'There are two bodies.' He nodded in the direction of my neighbour's house at the end of the street.

Joshua gave a small nod before he looked at me. 'Do you know what happened to them?'

I shook my head. 'Dad and I found them yesterday.'

'I'll take a look,' Geoffrey said. 'You go talk to your family.'

'Take a gun with you.' Joshua threw the shotgun to Geoffrey, who caught it cleanly.

Geoffrey frowned. 'One day you'll kill someone with your recklessness.'

'The gun's locked. Don't wet yourself,' Joshua retorted. Then he turned and passed one of the smaller guns to me. 'Ready?'

We approached my home. Dad had shut the door the day before, and I didn't have a key.

'Step aside,' Joshua demanded, aiming a revolver at the door. He shot twice. *What the hell?* I covered my ears—too late.

Joshua took a few steps back and threw himself against the door. It swung open, hitting the wall behind it with a loud bang. I walked forward but Joshua held me back. I raised my eyebrows at him.

'Let me go ahead,' he said.

Gun in hand, he had already moved into the house. I followed directly behind him, my own gun lowered but firmly in my grasp. Joshua glanced over his shoulder at me, before walking determinedly towards the steel door of the bunker.

'Do you have a key?'

'No.' Sudden panic made my voice sound high and weird. I *had* to get my family out of there, make sure they were safe.

I hammered against the door. The skin on my knuckles burned and it hurt like hell. Joshua stopped me, his touch gentle on my arm. 'If it's soundproof, they won't hear you.'

Fear shot through me. What if they weren't in the bunker?

'Do you have a spare key somewhere?' he asked.

The cookie jar! I rushed into the kitchen, my shoulder colliding painfully with the door frame. I climbed onto the counter and grabbed the jar from the highest shelf. Our set of spare keys was still in it.

Joshua leaned on the door frame. With his guns and hunting knife stuck in the waistband of his black jeans, he looked like the hunter that he was. 'Have you found it?'

'I think so—we need to try these,' I said, determined not to look at him.

After I'd tried the fourth key—which didn't fit— the door was opened from inside. Mom's worried face appeared in the gap and her eyes widened when she saw me. Before I knew what had happened, she'd wrapped her arms around me in a tight hug.

She smiled, but her face fell when she pulled back and caught sight of Joshua behind me. She took a step back, glancing between me and him warily.

Worry flickered in her eyes. 'Where's your father? And who's that boy?' she asked. Her voice had a hysterical edge.

'That's Joshua. And Dad...' My self-control crumbled and tears began to flow down my cheeks. Everything bubbled out of my mouth and my mother listened in horror.

Bobby came running up the stairs, but stopped abruptly when he saw my face. Mia tried to peek past him and her eyes widened when she caught sight of me. She'd never seen me cry before.

Mom clutched the banister. Her face was like ash and her breath caught in her throat. Desperate to calm her, I squeezed her hands. Another asthma attack could be too much. It had been getting steadily worse for months—she needed her medication.

Joshua glanced over my shoulder into the bunker, seeing my gasping mother, my scared brother and sister. His knuckles turned white from his grip on the revolver, his lips thinning out. 'Don't worry. Sherry and I will find him,' he said to my mother. He sounded more convincing than he had in the car.

Thank God.

Mom looked up at him and her breathing calmed. She gave a nod. Then she hugged him. 'Thank you for saving her. Thank you so much,' she spluttered.

Joshua winced and patted her back, before untangling himself from her grasp. I turned to Bobby. His lips were pressed together so hard they looked white. Our eyes met.

My fault that Dad had been taken by Weepers.

My fault that he might never come back.

All my fault.

It was there in his eyes.

I'd abandoned Dad. Even without the accusation in Bobby's stare, I knew that.

Mom ushered Bobby and Mia back down the stairs. I followed. Joshua stayed at the top of the steps, reluctant to set foot in the bunker. He clung to the banister, like a cat digging its claws into the ground to avoid a bath.

Mia leaped at me, her face lit up. I lifted her in my arms and pressed her against my chest as hard as possible without hurting her.

'We need to get going,' Joshua said. He slowly came down the narrow staircase and stopped on the last step. He looked around the bunker, his hand resting on the gun that he'd tucked back in his waistband.

'Where?' Bobby narrowed his eyes and crossed his arms in front of his chest. He straightened up to his full height, which was still only my height—a head smaller than Joshua, who he was obviously trying to stare down.

Joshua gave a small shrug, unimpressed by Bobby's macho antics. 'Where the Weepers won't hunt you down and gnaw on your bones.'

'Weepers?'

'Mutants.'

'And why should we trust you?'

I rolled my eyes at Bobby. 'Stop acting up.'

He opened his mouth, but Mom raised a finger. 'That's enough, Bobby. Let's not waste time. Your dad...' Her voice shook, and she stopped mid-sentence. She cleared her throat. '...needs their help.'

'It's Sherry's fault in the first place,' Bobby muttered. I flinched.

'Bobby! Don't you dare blame your sister.' Mom's

90

tone was final.

Joshua came up next to Bobby and looked down at him. 'I wouldn't want to see you fight two Weepers. If you were alive after that, then you could talk.'

To my surprise, Bobby stayed silent.

Joshua turned to my mom. 'Just take what you need with you. We don't have much time.'

Mia clung to my neck, her legs tightly wrapped around my waist. My arms protested, though she was nothing but skin and bones. I untangled her from my body and set her down. 'Help Mom pack our things.'

She gave an enthusiastic nod and dashed off. Grandma sat on the sofa, unperturbed by the events around her. She was knitting.

Click. Click.

No surprise there.

'Grandma, we're leaving,' I told her, in a voice I only used on her and Mia.

She looked up from the pompom hat she was working on. 'I won't abandon Edgar.'

Why couldn't things be easy for once?

Joshua looked at me and raised an eyebrow, mouthing the name. 'Edgar?'

'My grandfather,' I whispered. Not that Grandma would have heard me if I'd screamed—she was immersed in a tricky stitch. Joshua frowned and looked around the shelter. Of course, he couldn't see Grandpa.

'Listen, Erna, that's enough. We have to leave now. You can't stay here.' Mom walked towards Grandma and grasped her arm. Her face looked haggard, but she meant business.

'I can and I will. I won't come with you and nothing you say can change that.' Grandma shook Mom off

91

in an impressive display of strength for an old lady.

'Grandma,' I said as calmly as possible, but I could hear the edge in my voice. I kneeled in front of her feet. 'Grandpa is dead. I'm sure he won't mind if you come with us.'

Grandma smiled and patted my hand. 'I've been with your grandpa since I was your age. Where he stays, there I'll stay too. And if my time has come, then I'll rest next to him.' She patted my hand once more before returning to her knitting. Grandpa and Grandma had left Bavaria together and emigrated to the States a few years before Dad's birth. It had been Grandpa's idea, but Grandma always said she would have followed him to the moon.

Click. Click.

I wanted to rip the needles from her hand and hurl them at the wall.

Click. Click.

I cast a look over my shoulder at Mom—maybe she could convince Grandma. But she shook her head and lifted Mia into her arms. 'Fine, if she wants to stay here, let her stay.'

'Mom?'

She couldn't mean that. But she turned away and walked towards the steps. Why did it always fall on me to sort out any mess? I straightened up, struggling to keep my temper. Joshua came to my side, his posture tense. He really didn't like bunkers.

'Where's your grandpa?' he asked in a whisper.

'In the freezer.'

Joshua's eyebrows shot up. He looked at the huge freezer next to the sofa.

'He died six months ago.'

Joshua considered the freezer. Then he said, 'I think we can take your grandfather with us.' His voice was calm, as if he hadn't just suggested we travel with a dead body.

'What?' I stared at him. Was he serious?

He was serious.

He looked thoughtful. Maybe he was thinking of how best to manage it. Mom peered over her shoulder with an expression of disbelief. Her blonde eyebrows had nearly disappeared into her hairline.

Bobby walked up to us, glancing between me and Joshua, his eyes as round as saucers. His cool facade had slipped and the younger brother I'd dared to eat earthworms was back.

Joshua walked towards the freezer. He opened it and looked down—his expression giving no indication he was staring at a body that had been frozen for six months. Actually, it seemed to bother him less than being in the bunker.

Bobby, wanting to play tough again, walked up to Joshua and looked into the freezer with him. Grandma watched everything with a frown, but her hands didn't stop.

Click. Click.

I took a deep breath and forced my legs to carry me over to the freezer too. Don't look down.

My eyes darted down. Stupid idea. My stomach twisted and turned, my throat tightening. I looked away. This...thing...didn't look like Grandpa. Joshua moved closer. 'We can wrap the body in a blanket and put it in the trunk of Geoffrey's car. Then he can take it with them to Safe-haven.'

I blinked at him. 'Are you kidding?'

His blue eyes were grave. 'That, or we leave your grandmother here. It's your decision. But we need to hurry, or it might be too late for your father.'

Too late.

93

I gave a nod. 'Okay.'

Mom must have listened to everything, because she stared at us with wide eyes. 'What do you mean, "too late for your father"? It can't be too late! You said you could rescue him.' Her eyes darted between Joshua and me.

'It's fine, Mom. Don't worry. We'll bring him back. We just need to hurry and get everyone out of here. Even Grandma.'

I walked up to Grandma. 'We're taking Grandpa with us.'

That caught her attention and she put her knitting needles down. Wow, that was a first.

'Are we?' she asked.

'Yes.' I stripped one of the beds of its blanket. 'Take Mia and Bobby with you, Mom. We'll be right behind.'

'I'll fetch Geoffrey. We'll need his help.' Joshua rushed past my mother out of the bunker and returned with Geoffrey a moment later.

My mother greeted him with a brief handshake, before leaving the bunker with Mia in her arms and a protesting Bobby in her wake. If I'd been as pale as him, I wouldn't have played the tough guy.

Geoffrey looked around the bunker with a curious expression. His face brightened when his eyes landed on Dad's radio receiver.

'Does it work?' He stared at me like a child on Christmas morning.

I shrugged. 'I'm not sure. Until a few months ago we used it to talk to our neighbours, but since then the only sound coming from it has been hissing.'

Geoffrey nodded. 'Do you mind if I take it with me?'

'Sure. It's not like anyone's left who could use it.'

'Let's get the body out first,' Joshua interrupted, with a nod towards the freezer.

Geoffrey and Joshua began trying to lift Grandpa from the freezer. It took them a few minutes. He was stuck to the bottom and finally came free with a ripping sound. I retched. It didn't help that my stomach seemed to have moved to the back of my throat. Grandma watched everything with a faint smile on her wrinkled face. What the hell was there to smile about?

As Joshua and Geoffrey wrapped Grandpa in a blanket, they almost dropped him. Joshua made a desperate grab, accidentally wrenching a frozen, white arm out to ninety degrees.

I put my hand on Grandma's shoulder and steered her towards the staircase. She kept throwing glances at Joshua and Geoffrey while they carried Grandpa. She looked pleased.

'Mind the step,' I warned. With some gentle pushing, I got her upstairs. She'd even forgotten her yarn and knitting needles.

Mom, Bobby and Mia waited in the living room for us, staring at the soot-covered windows. I should have mentioned the bombardment. They would find out soon enough. Joshua and Geoffrey had hidden Grandpa's arm in the blanket and to my relief you couldn't tell what they were carrying. Mia would never realize that it was a body. I grabbed the handle of the front door.

'Gun!'

I jumped, my heart hammering in my chest. I glared at Joshua. Did he have to shout? I grabbed the gun from my waistband and opened the door a crack, weapon pointed at possible attackers. There was nobody around, except for a crow. It hopped

95

across the sidewalk, its black eyes fearless. It didn't even bother to fly away.

'Sunlight.' Grandma's face brimmed over with amazement. 'But tell me, Sherry, where are all the neighbours?'

'They're gone, Gran,' I said as I led her to Geoffrey's car. I made her sit down in the back seat, while Geoffrey and Joshua heaved Grandpa's body into the trunk and snapped the lid shut. Geoffrey hurried back into the house and returned with the radio receiver in his arms a few minutes later. He checked the wires and buttons as he walked, but managed not to stumble over his feet as he headed our way.

'It looks intact. Maybe I can get it running in Safe-haven,' he said excitedly.

Bobby, Mom and Mia stood on the lawn in front of our house. Their eyes were fixed on downtown LA. Or what was left of it.

Joshua looked at his watch. 'We need to hurry.'

Mom shook herself, then led Mia towards the car, while Bobby trailed behind them. He looked shaken. I was oddly calm. The sight of the destruction didn't bother me any more, though I knew it should. Perhaps Joshua was right. Maybe soon danger would be routine for me, like school and Izzy had been before.

1,142 days since the other life had ended.

'It's so quiet,' Mom said. Mia slipped into the back seat with Grandma. Bobby crossed his arms in front of his chest and jutted out his chin like he used to do when we battled for the last s'more.

'I want to come with you. I want to help.'

'No.' Mom's voice was firm. Final. She didn't even look at him. Her eyes were fixed on the remains of our hometown. 'You won't go with them. It's bad enough that Sherry risks her life...' A sob stopped her.

'Get into the car, Bobby,' I said, nodding towards the open door. Defiance crossed his face, but with another sob from Mom, it crumbled.

'Mom needs you,' I whispered.

He let out a low breath before he got into the car. 'Kick some ass, Sherry.'

I gave him a big smile as I closed the door. That was the Bobby I loved. Mom turned from the Los Angeles skyline and gazed at me, her lips quivering.

'Sherry.' Her voice broke. She cleared her throat, blinking a few times. 'I don't want to lose you, too.'

I forced a smile. 'You won't lose me, Mom. Joshua and I will find Dad and bring him back.' I opened the passenger door for her. 'Now get in the car. Geoffrey looks impatient.'

She sank down on the seat. Before she could say any more, I threw the door shut and ran to the other car. Joshua started the engine. Geoffrey's car headed off in the direction we'd come from. Back to Safehaven with my family. Well, what was left of it.

'Tired?' Grandpa turned the wire basket.

'Hmm.'

Bobby lay on his stomach, his mouth open, sleeping soundly. Grass and some stray leaves stuck to his hair.

I turned my head, my eyes searching the night sky. So many stars.

The soft rustling of the trees and the crackling of the campfire were the only sounds.

'You sure you don't want the last one?' Grandpa asked.

He pulled the stick from the fire. A droplet of chocolate dripped from between the graham crackers and into the flames. The fire sizzled, the flames reaching even higher.

Grandpa put the s'more on a paper plate and held it out to me. His eyes glimmered. He knew I couldn't resist.

The smoky smell of roasted marshmallow filled my nose. I grabbed the plate.

More s'mores. A motto Bobby and I lived by.

CHAPTER SEVEN

Our search for Dad could finally begin. But what if we didn't find him? I swallowed hard. We'd find him. We had to. The alternative was too horrific to contemplate.

The sun had risen and it was starting to get warmer. The Lincoln's air conditioning was broken, so we opened the windows. The air was fresh. Without millions of cars driving on the streets, the air quality had improved. No smog. It was the only good thing so far about this situation.

'Where are we going?' I asked into the silence.

Joshua reached for the glove compartment. His arm brushed my legs. I shifted, hoping he wouldn't notice my heated cheeks. His touch sent tingles through my body. I wasn't sure if it was from fear or Joshua's touch, but it felt strange to have feelings like this. He opened the glove compartment and brought out a map.

'Here.' He put it on my lap, patted it once, and returned his eyes to the street. 'I've marked places on the map where I've found lots of Weepers. I call those places nests.'

Nests.

I unfolded the paper and looked at it. It was a map of Los Angeles and its suburbs. My grip on the edges of the map tightened, crumpling the paper. There were a dozen crosses all over the map. So many of them. It would take for ever to search them.

'We'll check them all. The nests in Westlake and Jefferson Park are abandoned as far as I know, but we'll check them too.'

'Do you think they'll be there?' I asked.

'Probably. They tend to sleep during the day as far as I can tell. But some might be on the hunt. They're all very different. They even look different. Kind of like dogs, I guess. A Chihuahua and a Great Dane don't look alike, yet they're both dogs. It's the same with Weepers. Some look like furry beasts and some look almost like normal people.'

I tried to picture them. But I'd only seen one Weeper in the dim light of the supermarket. I'd never forget those wild eyes though.

'Karen said you hunt them.'

'I've been hunting them from the day I came out of that damn bunker.' His tone had hardened.

'Aren't you afraid? She told me that you've been injured before. They could kill you.'

Joshua looked at me as if the answer to my question was obvious. But it wasn't—at least, not to me.

'Sometimes, when I hunt them at night and feel them lurking in the shadows, waiting to attack, I'm afraid.' He shrugged as if it wasn't important. 'But then I think of everything they've done and about the people I might save, and anger wins over fear. They are killers. Sleep, eat, kill—it's all they do.'

I took a deep breath. His words were hard to stomach. He seemed to care so little about his own safety, his own life. 'Have you saved people before?'

'I've brought a few to Safe-haven. Only Tyler survived though.'

'They all died?' My hands became clammy and I had to dry them on my jeans. What if Dad died? Would we be risking our lives in vain?

Joshua nodded. 'Some were badly injured and died from their wounds. Others died from the rabies. Some survived the rabies, but they changed.' He clenched his jaw. The only sign of emotion. 'They became Weepers.'

'What happened to them?' I held my breath, my nails digging into the fabric of my jeans. I had a feeling it would be horrible.

Joshua laughed darkly. 'What do you think happened to them? We couldn't keep them in Safe-haven and we couldn't let them go.'

I exhaled, the air leaving my lungs in a rush. My mouth went dry. 'You killed them?'

'Geoffrey or me. It wasn't as if we had a choice. They knew where Safe-haven was. They'd have returned and tried to kill everyone.'

I licked my lips but it didn't help with the dryness. 'You did the right thing.'

'Sometimes I'm not so sure. Killing Weepers that are prowling the street is bearable. But killing someone you've known as a person...' He trailed off.

We sat in silence for a moment. I shifted in my seat. 'Karen said Tyler was badly injured.' I started playing with the edges of the map.

'Yeah, Tyler was a mess. At first he was in some kind of delirium caused by fever. He muttered non-stop, but the moment he came around he stopped talking altogether.'

'What was he saying while he was unconscious?'

'He said one thing over and over again. 'Fence, there's a fence.''

'Fence? What fence?'

Joshua shrugged. 'Don't know. I don't think he does either. Tyler's a nice guy, but he's gone totally nuts. I was surprised when he made it. I thought he'd die. But Larry wasn't in much better shape

103

when he and Karen showed up at Safe-haven. She took care of Larry, and then when I brought Tyler, she did the same for him. Without her, they'd both be dead.' His voice had become soft as he spoke about Karen—he liked her. Maybe she'd taken the place of his mother.

I wondered what had happened to his parents, but didn't dare ask.

Joshua slowed the car. I noticed that most of the surrounding houses had been bombed. Some were burned down to the ground, while others were almost intact, with only their windows smashed. Debris littered the streets, forcing Joshua to steer the car around chunks of concrete in a zigzag.

I retrieved the gun that I'd put next to my feet and held it in my hands.

Joshua stopped the car at the kerb. There were other cars in front and behind us, so the Lincoln didn't stand out too much. Huge warehouses towered above the streets, their faded signs naming companies that no longer existed. Once this place had bustled with people doing their jobs in order to provide for their families. Now they were all gone. Jobs, people, families.

Joshua turned round and grabbed his backpack from behind his seat. He took out a hunting knife in a black leather sheath and handed it to me. 'Just in case a close-combat situation arises.'

Close-combat? The last time I'd fought—and won—had been against Brittany Ferris in junior high. She and her hyenas had laughed at me because I'd stepped on my floor-length skirt and ended up pulling it off in the process. The mortification of standing in my cotton panties in the school yard had given me the motivation to bust her lip. But Brittany

Ferris wasn't a Weeper—or at least, she hadn't been then. Who knew what had happened to her since the rabies? The chances were she hadn't survived, and the thought made me feel bad. I shook my head. This wasn't the moment to get lost in memories. I took the knife and tied the sheath to a belt loop on my jeans. Joshua gave a small nod of approval before handing me another pistol.

So many weapons—as if we were going to war. I showed him the gun in my right hand. Surely, I didn't need another.

'You'll need another one,' he said, as if reading my thoughts.

Going to war indeed. What had he called it? The survival of the fittest. I took it from him and slid it into the back of my jeans. He gave me a handful of bullets next. 'Put them in your pocket. And Sherry—' He stopped me with his hand on my arm. 'Use them wisely. We don't have any to waste.' Before I could consider what his words meant, he continued. 'Do you know how to load a gun?'

'My dad taught me.' I stuffed the bullets into my pockets, hoping Joshua hadn't noticed how my voice had cracked. I pasted on a smile.

His gaze was intense, as if he could see right through me. 'Then let's go.' He got out of the car.

I followed, scanning our surroundings. The area seemed peaceful. I'd expected Weepers to lurk at every corner, waiting to attack. Weepers that were once people like you, a tiny voice in my head reminded me.

'Sherry?'

I jumped and glanced at Joshua, who'd walked a few steps towards one of the intact warehouses.

I sprinted after him. 'Are they in there?' A part of

105

me wanted them to be, so I could save Dad. The other part was scared witless.

'No, not in that one. But there's a smaller warehouse right behind it. They should be there. At least, they were the last time I was here.'

Goosebumps rose on my skin as we crept past the huge building. It cast shadows on us and our surroundings. Despite the shade, the air was stuffy and I began to sweat. I wiped my right hand on my jeans, then my left, trying to dry my palms. Joshua was a few steps ahead, his tall frame obstructing my view. He stopped and I almost bumped into him.

'What is it?' I asked, looking around for a sign of attackers. My hands wouldn't stop shaking. He shushed me and scanned our surroundings with narrowed eyes. He pointed his revolver at the door of the warehouse, which stood open a crack. It was too dark inside to make out if there was someone in there. I squinted against the sun, raised my own gun and aimed it at the same spot.

Nothing.

The wind picked up, giving us some relief from the heat. It also jolted a corrugated sheet roof somewhere, filling the silence with its clattering.

Joshua relaxed his stance. 'I thought I saw something move. Must have been my imagination.'

I lowered the pistol and took a shaky breath. Bobby and I had loved to play Cowboys and Indians when we were younger. Creeping up on each other had been fun back then. This wasn't fun at all. One wrong move, one careless moment, and Joshua and I would end up dead. This wasn't a game. I followed Joshua towards the smaller warehouse.

Silence. Shouldn't there be noises if Weepers and

106

their prey were in there? Screams, or maybe roars?

We reached the entrance to the warehouse, a heavy steel door. The metal sheeting of the building was completely covered in dirt and soot. My gaze lingered on the places where there were claw marks. Huge claw marks. Maybe it was just an animal. *Right*. I wished.

Joshua gave the door a small kick with the tip of his sneaker. It swung open with an ear-splitting creak. If anyone—or anything—was in there, they knew about us now. With the bottom of my T-shirt, I wiped the sweat from my forehead. I was sweating too much. Joshua didn't seem to be as bothered by the heat. 1,141 days in the air-conditioned bunker had really taken their toll. I already felt a hair's breadth away from heatstroke.

We entered the warehouse—one cautious step after the other. The heavy smell of burned rubber clogged my nose. It was very dark in the building. The thick layer of soot covering the windows high up in the walls blocked out most of the light. Why couldn't the bombs have smashed them in? Shelves with buckets and piles of tyres obstructed our view even further, but I was pretty sure we were alone. Or maybe I just hoped we were. Wishful thinking wouldn't keep us safe.

Joshua waved me closer when I fell behind, and I hurried towards him. Our arms brushed as we scanned the vast hall.

'We should check the back,' he whispered.

We crept further into the room. An acidly sweet smell filled my nose. A scent I'd encountered once before. I froze. It smelled like the bodies in front of our neighbours' house.

Please don't let it be Dad.

18 hours and 37 minutes since he'd gone missing. 67,020 seconds in the claws of Weepers.

A bang resounded through the warehouse and our surroundings were plunged into deeper darkness. I let out a cry. There was barely enough light to see Joshua, who stood right beside me.

We weren't alone. Something had closed the door. My heart felt like it would burst out of my chest. The pounding of my pulse seemed to fill the silence and my breath came in short gasps. Was this how Mom felt during one of her asthma attacks?

I felt for Joshua's arm. He didn't move, but his body was shaking. I wasn't the only one who was scared. Somehow, that wasn't reassuring.

Something was lurking in the darkness, stalking us. Ready to attack.

I aimed the pistol straight ahead and resisted the urge to sneak a peek over my shoulder. I wouldn't be able to see much anyway.

Joshua moved next to me, but I didn't let go of his arm.

Gunshots rang out. I tried to cover my ears, releasing Joshua's arm in the process.

The windows burst into pieces and sunlight streamed into the hall. I scrunched up my eyes against the brightness.

A scream tore itself from my throat. Raw and scared.

I shot.

Once. Twice. Three times.

There were at least three Weepers in the warehouse with us. Three that I'd seen. If they lived in the dark, their eyes were probably better than ours. Who knew how many more were hiding in the shadows of the tyres or crouching behind one of the piles? But

108

however many there were, they were watching us.

Joshua shot again and screamed something I didn't catch. My ears were ringing from the gunshots. Tears and sweat burned in my eyes. I couldn't see Joshua anywhere. He had disappeared into the shadows.

This is the end. The thought kept repeating itself in my mind like a never-ending mantra.

The end.

From the corner of my eye I saw movement and whirled around. I shot until there weren't any bullets left. I grabbed for the other gun in the back of my jeans, but my hands were sweaty and slipped off. Wheezing, I tried again.

'Sherry!'

I wrenched my head around. A creature—furry-faced and snarling—was coming for me. I heard Joshua loading his gun as fast as he could. *Click. Click. Click.*

I shot twice at the Weeper and missed both times. My hands shook so much I wouldn't have hit a target twice the size.

Concentrate, Sherry.

My third shot hit the creature in the shoulder. Strips of dead skin fell off its body, leaving glaring red flesh. It didn't slow down. More gunshots cracked in the warehouse, followed by roars and whines, and something that resembled a human cry.

Joshua? Where was he?

Determination burned through me. I managed to hit my target twice more, in the chest this time. The creature stumbled and dropped to the ground. It raised its head a few centimetres and looked at me with eyes that were too intelligent to belong to an animal. Milky tears poured out of its eyes, sticking

109

to its fur.

Weepers. I wished the name wasn't so fitting. But it would have killed me. It was either the Weeper or me, and I'd made my choice. Yet it had been a person once. Maybe a dad, or mom.

Stop it!

I pulled my eyes from the dying creature and looked around. Where was Joshua? My throat tightened, as if invisible hands were choking me. I grabbed a few bullets and loaded both guns as fast as possible.

'Joshua?' I shouted, my voice quivering. 'Joshua!'

Footsteps came closer. Clattering. Something shattered on the ground.

I took aim.

Joshua came running out between two shelves. His right sleeve was torn and blood was dripping down his arm. I pointed my pistol towards him—I'd shoot whatever was chasing him.

'Get out of the warehouse!' His chest heaved. 'There are more behind me.'

I whirled around and bolted towards the closed door. Joshua caught up with me. Piles of tyres had been thrown over and were rolling through the warehouse, casting twisting shadows on the walls. There was movement everywhere. I couldn't tell the Weepers from the tyres. Dust filled the air, making me cough. Joshua's legs were much longer than mine—he could have run faster—but he matched my pace. We jumped over tyres barring our way and dodged the ones rolling towards us. I was panting when we reached the door. I tried to open it, but it was stuck. Or the Weepers had blocked it. I jiggled the handle as hard as I could, hammered and pushed until my hands burned.

110

It didn't move. Not a centimetre.

Joshua turned and shot bullet after bullet. The gunshots no longer hurt my ears. I risked a look over my shoulder. Five Weepers pelted our way, shoving each other and ripping skin off in their greed to reach us. Two were moving on all fours, the others upright like humans.

I kicked the door and threw myself against it, while Joshua kept firing. Pain shot through my arm. Desperately we crashed against the door together, and it swung open. I fell to my knees and dropped the gun.

Sunlight blinded me. Joshua gripped my arm and pulled me upright, still shooting. I glanced behind us. Only three Weepers were left standing, but they were close. His hand clasped mine as we ran, dragging me behind him. It was difficult to keep up with his pace. Without his grip on my hand I would have fallen. Every muscle in my body protested.

The Weepers followed us out of the warehouse, but in plain daylight they were easy targets. Joshua shot another one. The ones left stopped chasing us and disappeared from view.

'Where are they?' I panted, my eyes searching our surroundings.

'Hiding. They must have realized that they don't stand a chance against our guns.' He gasped for air. We didn't stop running. Hot air filled my lungs with every ragged breath. It burned.

It wasn't long before we reached the Lincoln. We jumped into the car, grateful for its protection. The engine roared to life and we sped off in a cloud of burned rubber.

We'd gotten out of the warehouse alive, were safe

111

for now, but my body didn't stop trembling. Maybe because I knew this wouldn't be our only encounter with the Weepers.

Pushing the blanket away, I rolled onto my back. Beads of sweat glittered on my skin.

The door opened and Mom entered, carrying a tray.

A soft scent wafted over to me. Chamomile and honey.

Mom perched on the edge of the mattress. 'I made some tea for you. It'll calm your stomach.'

Her hand was so wonderfully cool. My eyelids drooped as if an invisible force was dragging them down.

'Sherry, you must drink.'

I forced my eyes open and eyed the cup. It didn't smell bad, and I liked chamomile tea. She brought the cup to my lips.

I took a gulp. The tea was hot, but not scalding. Mom always made sure I didn't burn my tongue.

I waited for my stomach to revolt and inched a bit closer to the bucket next to my bed, just in case. But nothing happened. A feeling of warmth spread through my insides. I relaxed against the pillows and smiled when Mom kissed my forehead. 'The public health officer will be here soon. Get some sleep until then, sweetheart.'

CHAPTER EIGHT

I leaned my head against the seat and took a few deep breaths. The stabbing pain in my foot brought tears to my eyes. The painkillers had worn off. Joshua winced as he steered the car. He was bleeding from a long gash on his upper arm and blood trickled down his tanned skin, dripping onto his jeans and the steering wheel. I twisted in my seat to take a closer look.

He glanced at me from the corner of his eye. 'It's just a scratch.'

'Doesn't look like a scratch to me.' I lifted the shredded sleeve and inspected the wound. It wasn't deep as far as I could tell, but I wasn't a doctor.

'There are a few belts behind the passenger seat. I keep them in case I need a tourniquet.'

I reached behind my seat and felt around for one of the belts. My eyes swept round the car, searching for something I could use as a dressing.

'Glove compartment,' Joshua said through gritted teeth. The first sign he was in pain.

There was something in there that looked like it could be used as a bandage. It must have been a shirt once, before someone had ripped the fabric into long strips. It looked clean, but anyway, it was all we had for now.

I rolled up Joshua's sleeve and began winding the strip around his upper arm. He clenched his jaw, but didn't complain. We were still driving at an insane speed. The seats creaked like they would break loose and catapult me through the windscreen. A hint of burned rubber hung in the air. If the tyres exploded, we'd be stranded in the middle of nowhere. I tried not to pay attention to the houses rushing by.

'How did it happen?' I asked while I fastened the bandage with the belt. He winced. 'Too tight?' I glanced at him.

He shook his head. 'I followed two Weepers into an aisle but I didn't pay enough attention. One of the Weepers sneaked up on me. It nearly got me. I managed to hit it with a bullet but the damn beast crashed into me. I was thrown against a shelf and something sliced open my arm. Are you done?'

I nodded and released him. The belt kept everything in place and the blood had stopped dripping down his arm. He looked down at the improvised bandage, then gave me a smile. 'You're a talented nurse. Perhaps I should keep you around.' He laughed and winked at me.

His cheeriness was so strange. We'd barely escaped the warehouse alive. Maybe he was just good at hiding his anxiety.

I leaned back in my seat. 'I thought they were going to get us.'

'We need to be more careful next time, and we need to do something about your aim.'

'What's wrong with my aim?'

'It's miserable.'

I narrowed my eyes. Miserable? At least I'd shot one Weeper. Before yesterday I'd never tried to hit a living target.

Joshua looked at me with a lingering smile. 'I don't mean to offend you, but it's in both our interests if you do better next time. The Weeper was running straight at you and it took you two gun-loads before you killed it. We're running out of bullets. Every shot has to be a hit.'

I slumped in my seat. 'I didn't want to kill it. Its eyes…' I trailed off. 'Its eyes looked so human. Like it was crying.'

Joshua reached over and took my hand. 'It was hard for me the first few times. But you get used to it. You don't have a choice. I don't like killing anything. I hate this life, the killing—but if it's not their death, it's ours.' He paused, drawing in a deep breath. For the first time I could see how difficult this life was for him. 'They're hunting us. Killing them is our only chance for survival.'

I stared down at our hands. His sun-kissed skin was light-brown, while mine was pale from the years in the bunker. I liked the sight of our entwined fingers, like honey and milk. Joshua gave me a sideways glance, and when he noticed my eyes on him he pulled his hand back, curling his fingers around the steering wheel. I missed his touch.

Joshua avoided looking at me after that. He seemed distant. I didn't get it. He'd taken my hand, not the other way around. Not finding Dad was bad enough, but Joshua's sudden coldness made it even worse. His moods changed even faster than Bobby's.

The strained atmosphere and the disappointment of not finding Dad—of not even having a clue where he was—pressed down on me like a heavy weight, until it felt like I had to squeeze out every breath.

*   *   *

We checked two more nests after the warehouse, both in south-eastern districts, but they were deserted. It looked like the Weepers had given them up long ago.

As evening fell, we began searching for a place to

spend the night. I didn't want to stop looking for Dad. Time was running out—if he was even still alive. I wanted to go on until we'd found him. I *felt* like I could go on for days without rest, food or water, running on adrenalin and worry alone, but it was too dangerous. Outside at night, we'd be easy prey.

'Maybe we should spend the night in one of the public bunkers?' I asked. It was the first time that I'd spoken more than one or two words since Joshua's change of mood.

His body tensed and a muscle in his jaw twitched. He glanced at me, then turned away. 'I don't think we should.'

I crossed my arms and leaned back. What was going on with him? 'Why not? We'd be safe there. Even Weepers can't burst through steel doors.'

He shifted on his seat and gripped the steering wheel with white knuckles. I waited for him to reply, but he just stared ahead. I kept my eyes on him, determined to get an answer—preferably an answer that consisted of more than one word.

'Fine!' He glared at me. 'We'll spend the night in a goddamn bunker.'

He dropped his left hand from the steering wheel and then ran it through his hair. 'Listen, I'm sorry. I didn't mean to yell.'

'It's okay. I just don't get you sometimes.' I shook my head, then shrugged, unsure what else to say.

'I'm used to doing this alone. It's easier.'

I felt like I'd been slapped. 'I'm sorry for being a burden.'

He groaned. 'You aren't a burden. That isn't what I meant.'

'It sounded like you did.'

He shook his head. 'You wouldn't understand.'

'Try me.'

He laughed. There was nothing happy about it. 'Have you ever lost someone you should've taken care of?'

'Are you kidding me?'

Realization flashed on his face. 'I forgot about your dad. But it was his job to take care of you, not the other way around. He's the adult.'

'I went with him to make sure he'd return to our family safely. I should have helped him, but I couldn't.' A lump rose in my throat. 'I abandoned him.'

'No, you didn't.' Joshua's face was set. 'You fought. You tried to help him, and even now you're risking everything to save him.'

I wanted to believe him. But I couldn't stop blaming myself. My throat tightened again. Maybe if Bobby had gone with Dad, it would have been different. I sucked in a deep breath, then peered at Joshua. 'I know what it means to lose somebody I should've taken care of. Now tell me what this has to do with anything.'

'When I'm on the hunt alone, I risk my own life, and if I fail, it's only my life at stake; only I pay the price for my mistakes. But with you, there's much more to lose. My failure can mean your death. It would be my fault.'

'You aren't responsible for me. It's my father we're searching for. You're helping me. You're risking your life, though you've got no reason to. If anything happens to me, it'll be my fault, not yours.'

'Do you think it's that easy? I'd blame myself no matter what you say.'

I knew it wasn't that easy. I blamed myself for

119

Dad's capture, and even if Joshua told me not to, I'd never forgive myself if we didn't find him.

'I can take care of myself. We'll both be fine. We'll find my father and then we'll return to Safe-haven. Everything will be fine.' My voice was full of conviction I didn't feel.

'Yes, it will,' Joshua agreed.

We sat in silence for the rest of the drive.

Joshua pulled up in front of a public library. It was built of white stone, and the lawn surrounding it had been neat and beautiful once. Now the grass was overgrown and weeds covered the paths. At least bombs hadn't destroyed it.

'There's a bunker beneath the building.' Joshua nodded towards the main entrance.

He grabbed the backpack from the back seat, before handing me bullets and a new pistol. I'd lost one of the two he'd given me this morning. If I carried on like this, we'd run out sooner than Joshua thought.

We got out of the car and checked our surroundings. A group of ravens had gathered on the sidewalk, screeching and pecking each other. Red flashed between them. They fought over what looked like a lump of flesh. Maybe just a dead cat. At least I tried to convince myself that's what it was. I definitely wouldn't check.

I stayed at Joshua's side as we approached the entrance to the building. His presence made me feel safe, though safety was an illusion in this new world.

'Were you in this bunker?' I sneaked a peek at him.

His jaw tightened. 'No. My family and I were in the shelter near the harbour.'

His family. I'd just opened my mouth to ask about

120

them, when I saw huge letters on the wide wall in front of me.

Judgement Day has come. Thou shall receive Our Holy Father's judgement gratefully.

The sun was setting, the orange of its fading rays making the facade glow.

'Gratefully?' Joshua snorted. He rolled his eyes at the message on the wall.

My attention was distracted by distant buzzing. It sounded like a swarm of bees. I searched the sky until I spotted a black dot. There it was again. Was it following me? Before I had time to look closer, the spot was gone. I stared at the darkening sky, hoping for another sign of the strange black thing. With a sigh, I turned away.

The wooden double doors of the library were wide open, but there was nothing welcoming about them. A trail of dried blood led up the grey stairs into the entrance hall. Withered leaves and twigs covered the granite floor. Layers of dirt caked the once-white stone, and several of the windows were broken. Shards lay everywhere.

'Come on.' Joshua nodded in the direction of another staircase leading down to the floors below. A sign announced that the restrooms were situated downstairs.

I clutched the pistol as I walked down the steps. The place smelled of urine and excrement. And iron. Blood.

Joshua moved towards a steel door that stood open. I paused next to him and peered into the darkness.

'If the generator isn't broken, we might even have light,' he said, flipping the switch.

The lamps in the bunker flashed, illuminating the

121

room. It was bigger than our bunker, but smaller than I'd expected. Beds, blankets and pillows lay all over the place. Twenty people could have lived in this place comfortably. Thirty would have been a tight fit. As I counted the beds, I realized at least sixty must have found shelter here.

No wonder fights had broken out in public bunkers. There was something oppressive about the air, as though the breath of sixty people still filled the room, their body heat turning it into a furnace, their hushed whispers like static. I could see them in my mind. Huddled together like pigs in a slaughter truck. No water. No food. Only chaos.

I descended the narrow staircase, my eyes sweeping over the mess. Joshua stood next to the door. He hadn't moved a centimetre.

'Joshua?' I kept my voice soft.

He started, and his blue eyes found me. He seemed to take a deep breath before he closed the heavy door behind him and locked it. Nobody would be able to open it from the outside. We were safe from Weepers and maybe we'd even manage to get a few hours of sleep. Slowly, Joshua came down the staircase into the bunker. He routinely hunted Weepers, and agreed to search their nests to find my father, but this bunker scared him. What had happened in the hundreds of public bunkers across the country? What had happened to Joshua? He stood beside me, the backpack with the guns and our food clutched in his hand.

'Are you alright?' Despite his tanned skin, he looked pale and his eyes were haunted. Questions burned on my tongue. Questions I wasn't sure I should ask.

We gathered a few blankets and pillows, and put

122

them on two beds that weren't broken. Then we pushed the beds next to each other against the wall furthest from the staircase. Joshua sat down on the nearest mattress, his back against the wall and his legs dangling over the edge. He put his backpack beside him. Two guns lay in his lap while he fidgeted with the hunting knife.

I slid off my sneakers and sat too. My wound had started bleeding and my right sock was soaked with the blood. I'd strained it too much. There was nothing I could do about it now.

I stole a glance at Joshua. He was staring at the knife in his hand, a frown creasing his forehead. Strands of blond hair fell into his eyes, but he didn't bother pushing them away. He looked lost.

The growling in my stomach disturbed the silence. Joshua rummaged in his backpack and produced the bag of biscuits and apples. He passed it over to me without a word, keeping an apple for himself. He took a bite and chewed carefully. His shoulders were stiff, his expression guarded.

I picked a biscuit from the bag. Licking my lips, I cleared my throat, attracting Joshua's attention. The blade of the hunting knife glittered under the glare of the halogen lamps as he twisted it absent-mindedly. I realized how close we were—together on a bed. Mom would have a seizure if she knew I was alone at night with a boy.

I took an apple and turned it in my hands. It gave me something to distract myself with. 'You seem to dislike being in bunkers.'

'If you'd seen what I've seen in a public bunker, you'd understand.'

I wanted to reach out and take his hand. I wanted to comfort him, but I wasn't sure how he'd react. He pulled his legs up and wrapped his arms around his knees, then rested his head on them. Obviously, he didn't want to talk about it. I wouldn't force him. Not that I thought I could. I ate the apple and put the stem down on the ground, then lay back on the bed. The pillow smelled dusty, making my nose tickle. I held the pistol to my chest and closed my eyes. The only sound was our breathing.

'Night,' I said.

There was no reply.

*   *   *

A scream ripped me from sleep. I jerked into a sitting position and grabbed the back of my head as pain shot through it, feeling the stitches and the tender flesh. Blinking rapidly, I tried to get used to the brightness. My fingers hurt from grasping the pistol so tightly.

Where had the scream come from?

Joshua lay on his side, twisting and turning on the bed, his face pulled into a grimace. Beads of sweat shone on his forehead, making his hair stick to his skin. He thrashed out with his right arm, as if fighting an invisible opponent.

'No.'

The word was nothing but a moan. I pushed my blanket back and crawled to the edge of my mattress, unsure if I should wake him. He began muttering under his breath. Tears glistened in the corners of his eyes. I reached a hand out hesitantly in his direction.

'No! Zoe!'

I froze. Zoe? His sister? Girlfriend?

He was thrashing so much that he nearly fell off

124

the bed. I leaned over and nudged his shoulder gently. His eyes flew open and with lightning speed he pinned me to the bed, his knife at my throat. The cold blade pushed against my skin. With every beat of my heart, it seemed to dig harder into my throat. I didn't dare move, or breathe or swallow.

He's going to kill me.

His eyes widened and he pulled back the knife. He let go of my shoulders and blinked, still kneeling over me. 'I'm so sorry, Sherry. I thought...' He trailed off, his eyes searching me. 'Have I hurt you?' He backed away until he was on the foot of the bed, giving me room to move.

I pulled my legs against my body and took a shaky breath before I shook my head. 'I'm fine.' My voice was a whisper.

His hand trembled as he ran it through his sweaty hair. 'Damn it. I could've killed you.'

'But you didn't.' I propped my chin on my knees as I looked up. With trembling fingers, I wiped a few tears from my face, hoping he wouldn't see them.

'Why were you on my bed?'

'You were having a nightmare.'

Something registered in his eyes and he looked away, embarrassed.

'I was dreaming about my time in the bunker... and about my family.'

I moistened my lips with my tongue. My mouth had become very dry. 'Where's your family?'

I knew the answer.

Joshua ran the blade of the knife over his palm. Then he looked up, and the expression in his eyes felt like a stab in the heart.

'They died.' His tone was flat, but his eyes showed so much pain.

'I'm sorry.'

Joshua nodded.

'You…you mentioned Zoe.'

Joshua turned and slumped against the wall. He pulled one knee against his chest. 'Zoe is…' He paused. 'Zoe was my sister.' His chin trembled. He swallowed and closed his eyes.

He looked lost again. I crawled over and sat beside him, clasped his hand in mine and squeezed. He let his head drop back until it rested against the wall.

'Was your family killed by…them?'

He let out a long breath and peered at me through half-closed eyes. 'My sister was. My mother…' He shook his head and squeezed his eyes shut as if he was trying to force an image out of his head. 'I don't know what happened to my father. He was in the military. He was supposed to pick us up after the situation had improved. But he never came.'

I blinked back tears. Silence settled over us. The air became stuffy. Suffocating. I couldn't bear it. Say something. Anything.

'Los Angeles seems deserted. Who do the Weepers hunt if there aren't any people left in the city?'

Maybe a happier topic would have been wiser.

Joshua didn't seem to mind the question. 'Just like your family, there are still people coming out of private bunkers. But as far as I know, the Weepers hunt animals, like wild boars and deer. They smell hot blood and body heat. Mammals. Birds. I've seen them kill and eat one of their own. Maybe they could live on vegetables and fruit if they chose to. But they prefer to kill us.'

'Maybe they see us as rivals.'

Joshua frowned in thought. 'Hmm. That might be

126

a reason.'

'It's scary to think that only a few hundred people might be left in North America.'

'I don't think that's the case. We had some contact with two other safe havens in California until our radio stopped working. The majority of the survivors left the cities and try to scratch along on their own in the country.'

His grip on the knife tightened, the veins in his hand standing out. I wanted to ask more about his time in the bunker, but the look on his face...

'Don't the Weepers ever leave the cities?'

He twisted the knife with a thoughtful expression. 'They seem to prefer the city. But maybe that's just the impression we get. They could be everywhere.'

'But they've never showed up near Safe-haven, or have they?'

What if Safe-haven wasn't as safe as we thought? My stomach clenched.

'No. Once a Weeper followed me, but I noticed it miles away from the house and shot it.'

It wasn't the answer I'd hoped for. The thought of a Weeper following Geoffrey's car towards Safe-haven made me sick.

Joshua looked at me and squeezed my hand. 'Your family is safe. Even if a Weeper came to Safe-haven, there are weapons in the house. Larry, Tyler and Karen are decent shooters. They'd kill the Weeper before it even reached the gate.'

'But what if the Weepers attack at night, when they're all asleep?'

Joshua smiled. 'Do you think we leave Safe-haven unguarded at night? There's always one of us awake.'

Maybe this news should have calmed me. It didn't.

'Is he the right guy for you?'

'Do we have to do that stupid quiz?' I let myself fall back on my bed. Izzy was immersed in the magazine and ignored me.

'First question…'

I let out a groan and threw an arm over my face.

'You met your crush: a) at a party, b) through your friends, or c) at school.'

'You know the answer to that question.'

Silence.

I peeked out from behind my arm. Izzy was watching me.

'At school,' I replied.

She smiled and made a cross at the right spot. She read the next question and made a cross.

'Hey, the questions are for me.' I tried to get a glimpse of the quiz, but Izzy hid it.

'Don't worry. You're too biased for that one.'

'Izzy! Give me the magazine.' I leaned over and snatched it from her hands.

She burst out laughing. 'You should see your face!'

CHAPTER NINE

My neck was stiff and even the tiniest movement hurt like hell. It felt like thousands of needles were pricking me, boring themselves through my skin and into my brain. My eyelids seemed to be glued shut. Ugh, I felt like shit. Thoughts from the day before flooded my mind. Dad was still out there alone. Was he hoping I'd come to save him or had he given up already?

I groaned and forced my eyes open, then screwed them shut because of the blinding brightness of the halogen lamps. Sleeping in a sitting position had been a bad idea.

I tilted my head to the side, ignoring the cracking of my neck. My eyes settled on Joshua's bed. He was gone. Fear shot through me. My gaze swept across the room. Nothing.

I stumbled to my feet. 'Joshua?' I reached for my pistol.

A creak made my finger tense on the trigger.

Joshua came through a door I hadn't noticed before at the end of the room. My grip on the gun loosened, my muscles relaxing, but then I froze. His hair was wet and dripping down his face and chest. Droplets glittered on his tanned skin. He was only wearing his jeans.

I'd seen bare chests before—at the beach when the guys from school had walked around in their swimming trunks. That wasn't what had me entranced.

Scars covered his body. Their white stood out against his butter-toffee skin. The longest ran from

131

his left shoulder over his collarbone. There were three scars of similar shape and length over his belly button. It looked as if claws had ripped his skin open.

I looked down when Joshua noticed me staring at his chest. A moment of charged silence followed and my skin started to tingle.

'There's a shower room. If you want, you can use it. But we'll set out in about thirty minutes, so you should hurry.'

His words made me raise my head. My lips parted. He was drying his hair with a blanket and had his back turned to me. I shivered. Over his shoulder blades was a tattoo. The word *Avenger* was written in italics on his skin. Before I could stop myself, I walked up to him and traced the letters with my fingertips. They were entwined and beautiful.

The muscles in his back rippled beneath my touch. He glanced at me over his shoulder. My stomach flipped and my cheeks grew hot, but I returned his gaze. 'Where did you get it?'

He wouldn't have been much older than Bobby was now when the rabies had broken out. It was unlikely that he'd had the tattoo back then.

'Tyler did it.'

'Tyler?'

He gave a small nod and grinned when he saw the look on my face.

'But where did you get a...tattoo gun?'

'I found the equipment in a tattoo shop,' he said with a shrug.

'And Tyler knew how to use it?' I wouldn't let someone with a tattoo gun near me, much less someone like Tyler.

'He was a tattoo artist in his other life.' He turned

132

around and pulled his T-shirt on over his head.

'How did you find out about his other life?'

'He wrote it on a piece of paper. It took weeks before I gained his trust.'

'Avenger?' I said curiously.

Something fierce flickered in his blue eyes. 'Yes. You should shower now.'

I took a clean shirt from the backpack and hurried towards the shower room. Thoughts of Joshua's tattoo kept flashing in my mind while I washed the grime from my skin. I couldn't stop thinking about its meaning.

I returned to the main room of the bunker, where Joshua was sitting on his bed. My jeans felt heavy with sweat and dirt, but at least the shirt was clean. My foot hurt with every step. Hopefully it wouldn't stop me running.

Joshua looked up. He nodded towards the guns that lay beside him on the bed. Their steel shone in the artificial light.

'I've loaded them with most of the bullets we've got left. We'll need to be prepared.'

I took two guns and stuffed one of them into my waistband. It still felt surreal, like I was caught up in a bad western or horror movie. Only the horror was real. I'd actually killed something. A few years ago, I hadn't been able to bring myself to shoot anything more than clay pigeons, even when I went hunting with Dad. But now I would do anything to find him.

'Do you have enough bullets?'

I showed him the empty pockets of my jeans and smiled apologetically. 'Needed them yesterday.'

His grin made me all jittery inside. 'Horrible aim,' he muttered under his breath, but I caught it. He handed me a box of bullets and tossed me an apple,

133

then slung his pack over his shoulder and walked towards the staircase, glancing back to make sure I was following. Taking a bite from the apple, I limped after him. He hurried up the stairs, two steps at a time.

I waited behind him as he unlocked the door and pushed it open. The smell of excrement and urine wafted over us and made me retch. I breathed through my mouth while we walked up the stairs to the ground floor. The acrid sweet odour lingered in my nose, as if it was burned into it.

The entrance hall of the library was much cooler than the day before. Not too warm and not too cold. I saw the reason for the change of temperature when I gazed out of the open door. Heavy, grey clouds covered the sky and the soft drumming of raindrops filled the silence.

1,143 days since I'd seen rain. Since I'd felt it on my skin. Since I'd smelled it.

The scent was fresh. It filled my lungs. I ran outside, raised my head and closed my eyes, letting the drops splash against my face. Better than a shower. Refreshing. Laughter bubbled up...but then died as fast as it had come. I shouldn't laugh, not in a situation like this. Not when Dad was still in danger.

'Sherry, come on!' Joshua's voice was almost drowned out by the rain.

I dipped my head. He waited next to the Lincoln, his arms crossed and a blond eyebrow raised. His hair was plastered to his face and his shirt clung to his body. He didn't seem as enthusiastic about the rain as I was.

I hurried towards the Lincoln. 'It's been so long since I've seen rain.'

134

He shook his head and got into the car. I slipped into the passenger seat. Joshua shook his head like a wet dog, sending droplets of water flying my way. I threw up my hands to shield myself.

'I thought you liked rain.' His cheeky grin made me want to punch him. I tried to hide my smile.

He fetched the map and pointed at the places we'd check next. Most were situated around the harbour area and one of the nests was in a park.

I shivered. Joshua tipped his index finger against the cross in the park. 'We'll go there last. The park's overgrown with brushwood and grass. It's probably the most dangerous area to search. Let's hope he isn't there.'

He started the car. The soft purr of the engine competed with the sound of fat raindrops pelting down on the roof and windshield.

It took us about thirty minutes to reach the harbour. The destruction in this part of the city was minimal. Only a few houses had been damaged. Cracks formed in the concrete though—some so huge that small trees sprouted from them. Nature was reconquering what had once been hers.

Joshua parked the Lincoln next to a warehouse close to the water, probably to keep the Weepers from spotting it. I could smell the salty green scent of the ocean.

1,143 days since I'd smelled the sea, heard the soft splash of waves.

I shielded my eyes with my left hand and stared at the cruise ships anchored in the harbour—their past splendour was covered with green slime. Algae. Some smaller ships were overturned. None of them looked like they were seaworthy.

Before my family had gone into the shelter, there

135

had been reports about evacuation ships. Thousands of people had found shelter on them. I wondered what had become of them.

'Weren't parts of the population put on boats instead of in bunkers?' I asked.

Joshua stared out at the water. 'I've heard stories about that. I don't know what happened to the people on the ships. Nobody does.'

I let my gaze stray over the water, searching the horizon for something. 'Maybe they're still out there.'

'They would've run out of food long ago. I don't think they could've stayed on the ships for three years. Let's search the area.' Joshua changed the subject, tearing me from my thoughts.

We walked around the deserted harbour, guns ready. The rain had lessened. There were only scattered raindrops now.

The size of the harbour, with its many warehouses and containers, complicated our search. There wasn't a sign of the Weepers, but we didn't check every container or warehouse, not even half of them. It would have taken us for ever and it was time we didn't have—Dad might be dead soon. But I couldn't allow myself to think about that.

My fingers shook, but I didn't loosen my grip on the gun. The Weepers could be hiding anywhere. Even on one of the ships.

The six-storey building in front of us looked even shabbier than the rest. Most of the white paint had peeled off, leaving a dirty grey. Even before the rabies had forced people to leave everything behind, this building must have been vacant. It looked like it had been offices for a shipping company.

A trail of blood led inside. Red. Fresh. It looked

as if someone had been dragged into the building recently.

Suddenly, Joshua grabbed my arm in a crushing grip and dragged me towards him. Air rushed from my lungs in a gasp as his chest collided with mine. He pressed us against the rough facade of the building, his body tense. I frowned at him and opened my mouth, but he put his index finger against my lips. The touch made my stomach flip. Our chests were pressed against each other so tightly, I could feel his heartbeat. I craned my neck to get a glimpse of his face. His blond hair was plastered to his forehead, the colour almost amber because of the wetness. Lines of worry showed around his lips.

It started raining more heavily again. The raindrops lashed against my face. Joshua leaned down and spoke quietly, his mouth brushing against my ear, his warm breath tickling my skin.

'They're in there. I saw one of them moving past a window on the second floor. It's a nest.'

I gulped noisily and stared up at him with wide eyes. 'Do you think my father's in the building?' I whispered.

'Perhaps. We need to get inside and search the rooms.'

I let out a shaky breath. The image of someone bleeding to death flashed in my mind. I couldn't let myself think it was Dad.

Joshua stepped back, giving me room to move. He crept along the facade, staying as close as possible to the building. I followed, trying to make no sound, but my stupid sneakers squeaked. I winced every time they did. My feet practically swam in them. What if the Weepers heard the noise?

We crept around the building to the back. There was a fire ladder leading up to the flat roof, but it didn't look stable. Joshua gestured to the ladder. I gave a small nod to show I'd understood. I looked up at the entire length of it—it looked as if a gust of wind could pull it from the wall.

Joshua started climbing with a look of determination, his steps not faltering even when the ladder creaked. I grabbed the handrail in a death grip, its steel cold against my skin, and followed after him. Within a few moments, I had caught up. My heart hammered in my chest, and every groan of the metal went right through me. A few times my sneakers slipped on the wet rungs, but I kept my balance and didn't fall.

We'd reached the third floor when the ladder creaked like it was going to fall apart. One of the rungs was loose and gave way beneath Joshua's foot. We both froze and listened. It was silent. Had the Weepers heard the rung snap?

We reached the roof within a few minutes. From there, we were able to look out over almost the entire harbour. In the distance, near one of the dockyards, I could make out movement.

Weepers?

I strained my eyes, but it was too far away to say for sure. I spotted an emergency exit on the other side of the roof and pointed at it to alert Joshua. He nodded, and began to sneak towards it. I followed, careful to keep my shoes from making a sound, and halted a few steps behind him. He wound his fingers around the handle of the door and pulled it open slowly. I held my breath and peeked into the building, half expecting a Weeper to pounce on me. Nothing but silence greeted us. A narrow staircase led to the floors below. We entered the building and closed the door, Joshua wincing as it clicked shut. I wiped the raindrops from my face with the back of my hand.

'We need to be absolutely silent. If they notice us too soon, everything might be over,' Joshua whispered, his eyes darting down the stairs.

'Okay.' I sounded as if I'd run a marathon.

We moved down the steps. The only light was coming from small windows along the stairway, but it was enough for us to make out our surroundings. I would see if something attacked us. At least, I hoped I would.

We got to the sixth floor and moved through a long corridor with dozens of doors. The linoleum floor muffled our footsteps. Dried blood covered parts of it. I was getting used to the sight. The humidity was stifling and the smell of wet dog hung in the air. I scrunched up my nose in disgust.

'We should stay together.' Joshua cast a worried look at me.

I gave a nod.

It took us nearly twenty minutes to peer into every room. They weren't furnished, so nothing could have hidden in them. No sign of humans.

On the fifth floor we didn't have much more luck.

We'd never find Dad like this. Side by side, Joshua and I stepped onto the fourth floor. The smell of wet dog and bodies was stronger here. I glanced at Joshua. He pressed a finger against his lips.

A whimper from nearby startled me, and I fumbled with my pistol. It had sounded like a human—like a scared child. My throat tightened and it became difficult to swallow. Joshua crept towards the door closest to us and opened it a crack.

139

After a moment he shut it with a shake of his head and moved to the next door. I followed and chanced a look past him into the next room.

A scream stuck in my throat. I scurried backwards until I bumped against the wall behind me, my pistol raised.

Joshua didn't move. He pointed his gun steadily at the Weeper that lay curled up on a stack of papers. It was breathing, but it seemed fast asleep. Or maybe it was just pretending to be asleep. It was wearing torn trousers, pinstriped with a crease. They might have belonged to a nice business suit once, many years ago. Bloody marks and scars littered its hairy back, and blotches of purple flesh peeked through the fur where skin had fallen off. I couldn't see its face, but I was sure it was more beast than human. I felt sad that a virus could turn a human being into a soulless monster. It would most likely kill us if it knew we were so close. It wouldn't show us pity, because it wasn't in its nature. Pity and compassion were human traits that Weepers had shed like their skin.

We should shoot it.

I stared at the sleeping creature again. It had been like Joshua and me once. Maybe I'd even known it.

It wasn't its fault. As long as it didn't attack us, I wouldn't be able to end its life. I couldn't.

I lowered my gun, but I didn't move from my place against the wall. Joshua stared at the Weeper too. Would he kill it?

Should I let him?

I hesitated.

To my surprise, he closed the door and turned to me.

'Too loud,' he mouthed, with a nod to the revolver

140

in his hand.

Of course. Every Weeper in the building would have heard a gunshot.

We tiptoed towards the next door. Fortunately, my sneakers had stopped squeaking. But my foot hurt with every step.

A door creaked, and I froze, but Joshua gripped my arm and pulled me against him. We pressed back against the door we were about to check next. The Weeper with the business suit stood in the corridor, a few steps away from us. It had its back to us and its breathing filled the silence with rattling pants, as if it had been a chain smoker in its other life. Every heave of its body made strips of dead skin sway.

The door frame was narrow and wouldn't hide our presence if it turned around. It didn't move, just stood there and stared down the corridor from where we'd come. I heard it sniff.

What if it smelled us?

I looked up at Joshua. His chest heaved against my back and his grip on my arm didn't loosen. He aimed the revolver at the Weeper.

A shuffling drew my focus back to the beast. It had taken a step back, closer to us. The dead skin looked like it belonged to a snake, and its spine looked strange. The vertebrae were too big and pushed against the skin as enormous white bumps. With every intake of breath they got more prominent, as though they might poke right through.

Like Karen had said, this wasn't just rabies. I'd seen dogs with rabies and they'd been aggressive and out of their mind, but they were still dogs. Rabies hadn't changed what they were. But this virus turned its victims into something else entirely.

Weepers were neither human nor animal. They

141

were something other. Something wrong.

A howl sliced through the silence. I jumped, my head colliding with Joshua's chin, the clunk loud to my ears. The Weeper straightened and responded with a similar noise before it dashed away and disappeared from our view.

We stepped out and Joshua rubbed his chin.

'I'm sorry,' I mouthed.

A whimper sounded in the corridor, setting my teeth on edge. It was coming from one of the doors further down the hall. Joshua and I exchanged a look and ignored the doors next to us. We hurried towards the whimpers and stopped in front of a white door. At least, it had been white once—now there were bloody handprints all over it.

The noises were getting louder. Desperate whimpers. They were coming from behind the door. I reached for the handle and pushed it down, but it was locked. Damn it! Stupid door. I jiggled the handle with more force. It didn't budge.

I kneeled down and peeked through the keyhole. All the air left my lungs. There were people in the room. Three, from what I could see, but my view was limited.

One of them looked like Dad, slumped against the wall with his eyes closed; a mat of red hair and a shiny freckled chest. Was it really him? Was he alive?

40 hours and 3 minutes of hoping and worrying and wishing. It seemed too good to be true.

I couldn't tell if he was breathing. My heart thudded wildly in my chest.

'My dad—I think he's in there.' My throat was painfully dry, I could barely speak, and my tongue got stuck to the roof of my mouth.

142

Joshua got down on his knees beside me and peered through the keyhole. He shook his head, twisting his hair in his fingers. 'There's three of them in there. They're probably badly injured. We can't save them all.'

I pressed my lips together, trying to hold back tears. 'We can't leave the other two behind!'

'We'll have to kick down the door, unless you have a better idea. The Weepers will hear and then they'll be after us. We won't have much time. If those people can't run on their own, they'll need our help and we won't be able to hold up more than one person each.' His eyes took in my face. What was he looking for?

My mind was a mess. I couldn't think straight. There must be a way to save them all. 'Can't you try to open the door with your knife? I've seen it on TV.'

'We can give it a try.'

Joshua pulled the knife from the sheath at his waistband and pushed the tip into the lock. He twisted it a few times, but nothing happened.

A noise on the floor below made us both freeze. We stared at each other, holding our breath. It sounded as if something was coming up the stairs.

'Move back,' Joshua ordered. I rose from my kneeling position and took a few steps back. What was he doing?

'We don't have time for experiments,' he hissed. He pointed the revolver at the door and shot twice. Then he kicked against it and it swung open. Every Weeper in the building knew we were here.

Joshua and I stormed into the room. The smell of decay made me retch. My gaze swept over two rotting bodies. Maggots covered them, digging their

143

fat, round bodies into the fleshy skin. If we'd found them sooner…

No time for this.

For them it was too late. The other survivors could still be saved.

It was Dad!

After 2,403 minutes, our search was over.

I rushed towards him. We'd really found him. My heart pounded as I shook his shoulder. His eyes fluttered open, but it took a moment before they focused on me.

'Sherry?' he croaked.

I gave him a weak smile. Relief. I wound my arm around his back. 'Can you walk?'

He stared at me as if he couldn't believe I was there. As if he was scared of it.

'Hurry up!' Joshua hissed.

I straightened up and helped Dad to his feet. He leaned heavily on me and I could barely support him. His right leg was covered in blood and a long gash ran across his upper thigh. The entire trouser leg had been ripped off. The skin was swollen and glaring red.

Joshua tried to wake a middle-aged man who lay on his back, mumbling incoherently. His face and chest were covered with wounds, blood and pus oozing from them. A few maggots had started feeding on him. Joshua gave up after a moment and wrapped his arm around a young woman with black hair who sat next to the man. She was thin and weak, but I couldn't make out any serious injuries.

Beside them, another man, maybe in his early thirties, rocked back and forth on his heels, his eyes wide and terrified. His brown hair was plastered to his forehead. He was able to stand and walk alone.

Thank God—neither Joshua nor I could have helped him.

I followed Joshua, the woman and the man out of the room. Dad tried to use his injured leg, but he winced every time. His skin felt impossibly hot. A fever. Or something worse. I couldn't think about that possibility now.

Footsteps rang out. Something was running in our direction. I accelerated my pace. Dad gasped for air, but I couldn't slow down.

Joshua began shooting behind him while he led the woman through the corridor. We were heading in the opposite direction from where we'd come.

I looked over my shoulder. Only three Weepers were following us. They were closing in fast, running upright like humans. But the noises coming from them weren't human at all. Their roars sent shivers down my back. I pointed my pistol, fired, and hit one of them in the stomach. It whined and fell to its knees, clutching its middle. Blood ran over its hands. I looked away. I hated doing this, hated this new world for forcing me to kill something. Tears blurred my vision, but I didn't bother wiping them off, didn't even dare look at my hands for fear of seeing blood on them.

We got to the window at the end of the corridor. It led out to a platform and another fire ladder. Joshua opened the window and gestured for the man to go first. The roars were nearer now. I didn't dare check how close the Weepers were.

I helped Dad onto the narrow platform, holding his arm the entire time in case he lost his balance. Heavy raindrops lashed us, soaking our clothes. We were four floors up. Joshua was still shooting bullet after bullet while I helped the woman out. She

145

swayed and grabbed onto the railing.

The platform didn't provide enough room for all of us. The brown-haired man stepped onto the ladder and began his descent. I followed. Dad was above me and grimaced with every step. He kept skidding on the slippery metal. The woman was a few steps above him—she wasn't faring much better. If they fell, they'd take me down with them.

Joshua stopped shooting and began climbing down the ladder.

'Are they gone?' I called up to him.

'Yes, but there'll be more,' he shouted over the wind. It had picked up and blew my hair against my face, obstructing my view and catching in my mouth.

A snarl sounded beneath me. My eyes darted down.

Two Weepers waited for us on the ground.

'Sherry, pay attention!'

I sat up with a start, the gun almost slipping from my grasp.

Dad pointed ahead. 'There. Do you see them?'

A few quails were searching the clearing for food. I gave a nod.

'Take aim, make sure your hand isn't shaking, then pull the trigger.'

I'd heard those instructions dozens of times, memorized them.

It was easy. Just a few actions.

And yet I couldn't move.

The quails moved towards the shrubbery. So unsuspecting.

'Sherry, fire. They'll be gone soon.'

I raised my gun. Took aim. Just a small twitch of my finger, then the quail would be dead.

It looked up as if it could see me, but we were too well hidden.

Run. Just run, you stupid chicken.

'Sherry!'

I flinched. A shot rang out, tearing through the silence.

Startled quails scuttled into the bushes.

'You missed them on purpose, didn't you?' Dad looked at me, a smile in his eyes.

CHAPTER TEN

Misty brown eyes locked on mine, pus-like liquid welling from its tear ducts and smudging its papery skin. Its face showed no emotions, only hunger and greed. There was nothing human about it. One of the Weepers snarled and flung itself at the ladder. The vibrations went right through me. My fingers clawed at the rain-slicked handrails. The second beast followed. Another jolt went through the fire ladder.

Too much.

The ladder tipped, its metal supports breaking from the wall.

'Hold on!' Joshua screamed. I hooked my arm around the handrail. My temples began to pound.

Tremors jolted the ladder. God, what could we do?

A scream tore through the rain. The man! His grip on the handrail loosened, his panicked eyes on the Weepers beneath him.

'No!' The cry rang in my ears.

It was too late. He fell down the ladder and landed on the concrete with a sickening crack. He lay sprawled out on the ground, his eyes wide and lifeless. A puddle of blood spread around his head. Purple on grey. My muscles slackened and my grasp on the handrail loosened.

Be strong.

My fingers closed around the metal. I aimed my pistol at the Weepers, then shot twice. They ducked and the bullets missed.

Damn, they were fast!

The woman above Dad began to scream. I grabbed the rail and leaned back to get a better view, but raindrops blurred my vision. I aimed again. A bullet hit one Weeper in the neck, sending scraps of skin flying. The tendons shining through its white skin tensed briefly, its hunched back warping even more, before its muscles slackened. With a shriek, it fell to the ground beside the human body.

The other Weeper had almost reached me. Its smell definitely had. Bitingly mouldy. Like a dirty, soggy washrag that hadn't been cleaned in months.

'Sherry, get out of the way. I can't shoot!' Joshua shouted.

Where should I go? Panic clawed at me, threatened to choke me. I shot a few more times at the Weeper. One bullet grazed its hairy arm, but didn't stop it. A snarl erupted from its chapped grey lips. The skin around its mouth tore further with every growl.

'Sherry! You're in the way!' Joshua sounded scared.

The pistol slipped from my hand. My horrified gaze followed its fall as it crashed to the ground. Merciless claws grasped my ankle, wrenching and twisting. I clutched the handrail.

Sharp nails pierced my skin. My ankle screamed. Hot, searing pain. I cried out. I'd die. I'd end up like the man, cracked open and sprawled out on the concrete.

'Sherry!' Dad screamed, Joshua too, and the woman was still shrieking.

Shrieks and screams and snarls and growls. And white hot agony.

I kicked out at the beast with my free foot. My sneaker made contact with its hairy face, tearing off a huge strip of skin. Almost human, except for the empty eyes. Spit was dripping out of its mouth and mixed with its tears. I kicked again and it roared, but it didn't let go.

Dad bent down and grabbed my arm to pull me up, but he was too weak. The beast still tried to drag me down.

'Use the other gun!' Joshua ordered.

I looked around in panic, kicking and struggling. The beast pulled back its lips, revealing yellow teeth. My next kick hit against its forehead and its grip loosened. I fumbled for the gun in my waistband, but my fingers only brushed against the cool steel. The ladder tipped. My feet slipped from the wet steps and I fell. My hand shot out, gripping. Stabbing pain shot through my arm, up my shoulder and down my back. The Weeper pulled at my leg. My fingers started to slip.

Three gunshots rang out in close proximity and a steely grip wound itself around my wrist.

Two bullets hit the beast in the head. It let go of my ankle and crumpled to the ground. I gasped for breath and looked up.

A tanned, strong hand held onto my wrist. Pink nails with white new moons.

Joshua.

He must have climbed past Dad and the woman. I regained my footing and grabbed the handrail with both hands. Our eyes met. There was something fierce in his. I managed to give him a smile.

I took a moment to compose myself before I dared to climb down the remaining steps. I gave the bodies a wide berth. They lay in a puddle of blood that the still-pouring rain was slowly washing away.

'Here.' Joshua handed me the pistol I'd dropped. 'Come on.' He led the woman away from the office building, half dragging her. I slung my arm around Dad's middle and helped him walk after them. He looked very pale, but he had a shaky smile on his face. 'Thank you for saving me,' he whispered in my ear.

'No need to thank me.' I kissed his cheek.

I breathed a sigh of relief when the Lincoln came into view. Joshua helped the others into the back seat before we both got in. When the engine roared into life, I slumped against the seat, only to freeze a moment later. Two Weepers were heading our way. Both were naked except for the hair covering almost every centimetre of their bodies. They snarled as they lifted their heads to sniff the air like dogs. Joshua pressed his foot on the gas and the Lincoln shot forward. He rolled down his window, pushed his head out and fired. We were speeding towards them at a crazy pace, Joshua barely paying attention to the wheel. The Weepers whirled around and scurried away.

'Joshua?' I dug my hands into the seat, balancing my pistol on my lap.

The woman on the back seat started shrieking again.

'Joshua? What are you doing?' I screamed.

'Hunting them.'

'Stop it!'

He ignored me and shot at the backs of the Weepers. They ran into a narrow alley that we couldn't enter with the Lincoln. He braked hard and before the car had stopped, he ripped the door open and leaped out. What the hell?

I skipped out of the car too and ran after him. He was fast and my foot was white hot agony. Had he lost his mind?

'Joshua!'

He threw a glance over his shoulder and jerked to a halt. His eyes flitted between me and where the Weepers had just rounded the corner of a warehouse.

I reached him before he could make up his mind to run after them. My hand clasped his. 'You can't just leave! We need you. My father and that woman need you!' Tears blurred my vision.

He stared at me unblinkingly, his shoulders slumping. 'You don't understand.'

'Because you never explain anything to me!'

He shook his head. 'Let's get back to the car. I've lost them anyway.'

I didn't let go of his hand. 'Maybe it would help you to talk with someone,' I said.

'Not here. In the car.' He slid into the driver's seat. I took my place beside him. The woman had pulled her legs up against her chest and was rocking back and forth.

Dad's eyes were closed and his breathing was shallow. I put my arm between the front seats and shook him gently. His eyes opened a slit and the corners of his mouth lifted, but then, as if smiling cost him too much strength, they dropped.

'How are Mom and the others? Have you seen them?'

I had to strain my ears to hear him.

'They're alright. They're somewhere safe.'

He gave the hint of a nod and closed his eyes. The engine came to life and the car shot forward. Within a minute, we'd left the harbour behind us.

'What was that about? Why did you follow them? They could have killed you.'

Joshua's voice was soft and quiet. 'I knew one of them. I've seen the taller Weeper before.'

I wanted to reach for him, but something stopped me. The empty freeway lay ahead of us, the grass peeking through the cracks.

'During one of your hunts?'

'No. When my sister died.'

'The Weeper killed her?' Images of hungry brown eyes flashed in my mind.

Joshua didn't reply, but tears glistened in his eyes. He wiped them away and stared out of the windshield. I covered the hand resting on his leg with mine. Would he ever tell me what happened to his family?

We kept our hands entwined and I slumped against the seat. Joshua glanced into the rear-view mirror. For the third time. Had he seen anything? His hands wound around the steering wheel and his posture tensed.

I shifted closer to him, sneaking a look at the back seat to make sure Dad and the woman weren't listening. No need to worry them unnecessarily.

'What's wrong?'

He gave me a fleeting glance before he checked the mirrors once more. 'I think some of them are following us.'

I looked out of the back window. An empty street and a clouded sky. Nothing else.

'Are you sure?' I kept my voice down.

Dad's eyes stayed closed and his mouth was slack. He was asleep or unconscious, but he was breathing. The woman beside him had her face buried in her knees. At least she'd stopped whimpering. They weren't paying attention to what was going on.

Joshua gave a nod, his fingers drumming on the steering wheel. 'They keep their distance because they don't want to alert us. But I've seen three of them. It's difficult for them to keep up with the pace

154

of the Lincoln, though.'

Three of them?

My stomach clenched. I sunk my fingernails into the worn-out leather of the passenger seat. Why couldn't those monsters leave us alone? What had we done to them?

Everything, I guess.

I reached for the pistol in the footwell where I'd dropped it, trying to force the thoughts out of my head. The cold metal felt too heavy in my palm. Joshua reached behind his seat for his backpack. Steering the car with one hand, he seized the shotgun.

It was strange how guns and shooting had become such a crucial part of my life. I had always despised violence, and still did, but now it seemed impossible to go without it for even a day.

During my time in the shelter, I'd longed for adventures. 1,141 days of boredom and routine. But after three days of fighting, hurting, bleeding, I wanted them back.

Joshua let his window down. Cool wind and raindrops blew into the car.

'Won't they follow our trail with the windows open?' I asked.

'They're already following us, so it's too late to cover our tracks. And your dad and that woman look like they could really use some fresh air or they'll pass out.'

The pistol lay heavily in my right hand. I lowered the window on my side and leaned my head out. Wind and rain lashed against my face, blinding me for a moment. I squinted.

'Be careful,' Joshua warned.

Something flashed between two bushes. Weeper.

'Take the shotgun,' Joshua said.

The woman on the back seat began screaming—had she ever stopped?—and Dad let out a low moan.

'What?' I blurted. My head whirled around. Joshua held the shotgun out to me in a steady grip. Why were my hands always trembling when his were as steady as a rock?

I glanced down at the gun and hesitated. I'd never used a shotgun. Could I handle it?

'Take it.' Joshua thrust it at me. I took it with trembling hands and a queasy feeling in the pit of my stomach. 'We can't let them find Safe-haven. They'd attack and we'd lose our home.'

I put the smaller gun on my lap and leaned back out of the window with the shotgun. Then I started shooting.

I shot every time a Weeper came into sight, but they were fast and clever. Wind moved the bushes and trees. The movements confused me.

In just minutes, I was almost out of bullets. If I didn't hit my targets soon, we'd be in big trouble.

A Weeper dashed out of the bushes at the roadside behind us and onto the freeway. I gasped, my finger twitching on the trigger. It was running on all fours, yet it still looked human. Strips of skin waved in the wind like crêpe paper. I took aim. Before I could pull the trigger, it disappeared into the brushwood. I shot at the bush until my bullets were gone. I fumbled blindly for the pistol on my lap and prepared myself to shoot again if something moved.

You've become quite the assassin, haven't you?

My grip on the pistol loosened and my breath stuck in my throat. I closed my eyes, trying to pull myself together.

156

Not by choice. If I could choose, I'd never kill a creature.

Why couldn't they leave us alone? Why did they have to force me to kill them? Part of me resented them for leaving me no choice, the other part felt crushed by guilt.

I hastily pushed those thoughts aside, and scanned the area. Where had the Weeper gone?

Everything looked peaceful.

'I can't see them.' I strained my eyes. The wind had changed direction and now kept tousling my hair, obstructing my view. I pushed the strands away, but they flew back into my face.

'I don't see them either.' Joshua sounded collected. 'Close the window. They might have given up. They can't keep up with the speed of a car for long.'

It began raining heavily once more. The first fat raindrops lashed against my face. I moved my head into the car and closed the window, but kept my eyes on the roadside. If anything moved in the bushes, I'd shoot it, even through the window. I glanced over my shoulder at the back seat, my eyes sweeping Dad's body.

Beads of sweat glistened on his forehead, his lips were parted and his breath came in shallow gasps. I touched his knee gently. He jerked and his eyes fluttered open with a look of fright. But they shut instantly. He looked so weak, so small. I wanted to hold him and make everything better, but there was nothing I could do. I felt so helpless. We needed to get him to Karen. She'd know what to do.

I shifted my attention to the whimpering woman beside him. Her body shook and her face was buried in her knees. The sounds coming from deep in her throat made goosebumps break out on my skin. My

157

heart went out to her. That was what this new world turned people into. Her skinny legs peeked out of her shorts, scratched and bloody.

I touched the arm that was wound around her legs. 'Hey,' I said gently, worried about scaring her. 'You're safe now. Nothing will hurt you.'

Her whimpering quietened and she raised her face a little to look at me with terrified eyes. They were rimmed red from crying and her pupils were dilated. I forced a smile, patting her arm. 'I'm Sherry. My family and a few other survivors are waiting for us at a place called Safe-haven.' My words seemed to calm her and her body relaxed. A fine sheen of perspiration covered her skin. Both my father and her seemed to have a fever. Were they infected? Fear shot through me, but I kept my expression neutral. No need to worry them.

'What's your name?' I got out, through the lump in my throat.

She blinked at me and licked her chapped lips. 'Rachel.' Her voice was raspy from screaming or lack of use. Her lips turned up uncertainly, as if she'd forgotten how to smile. No surprise in this new world. There weren't many things left to smile about. Her skin was very tanned and her eyes reminded me of dark chocolate.

1,143 days since the last Hershey bar had melted on my tongue—special dark with almonds. We hadn't bothered taking candy into the bunker.

'We'll arrive in Safe-haven soon,' I assured her, though I'd lost track of where we were.

I glanced at Joshua, who must have felt my eyes on him. 'I made a detour to get rid of possible pursuers, but we should arrive in a few minutes,' he said.

I leaned back against the seat. 'Are you sure that the Weepers aren't following us?'

'Yes, I'd never return to Safe-haven if I thought we were still being followed.'

I let out a sigh and rubbed my face. 'My father doesn't look well,' I said as quietly as I could manage.

'No, he doesn't.'

I wrung my hands in my lap. 'Do you...' I gulped. 'Do you think he's infected with the rabies?'

Joshua looked hesitant. 'I can't say. The sweating could be an indicator. But it could also be caused by an infection.'

'But what if he's infected with the rabies?'

'Don't worry yourself unnecessarily. Karen will check him and then we'll know more.'

But not worrying was easier said than done.

Mr. Flores droned on and on about the Boston Tea Party. His voice a purr, like the sound of the air con. I ignored him.

I shifted on my seat until I had a good view of the table two rows behind me. Alex was scribbling. His auburn hair fell over his face, hiding chocolate brown eyes.

If he'd just move a tiny bit, then I'd see him better.

I stuck the end of my pen in my mouth and started chewing.

Alex's head shot up. Our eyes met. I jerked the pen from my mouth. Attempted a smile.

He noticed me. For the first time in…ever.

Someone started snickering. The class stared at me.

Turning to the window, I checked my reflection.

Oh God.

I'd put the wrong end of the pen in my mouth and my smile was black and terrifying.

CHAPTER ELEVEN

The door of the house was thrown open before the Lincoln had even come to a halt. Mom and Bobby burst out, followed by Karen and Geoffrey. Larry limped a few steps behind, his glasses resting on top of his head. I leaped out of the car, stumbling in my excitement. Mom's eyes were wide and anxious.

'You're back! Oh thank God, you're back! Did you find him?' Her voice quivered as she hurried towards me.

She was dressed in ill-fitting clothes. Probably Karen's. They were still better than her own, with their holes and stains. The T-shirt was too wide and hung off her narrow shoulders. The grey trousers were held up by a black leather belt. She looked like the walking dead. Sunken cheeks, wan skin, hollow eyes.

'Yes,' I said.

She threw her arms around me and clung on, as if she hadn't seen me in months.

'I thought I'd lost you, too. I felt so guilty for allowing you to search for him. But you came back. You saved him.' She trailed off with a small sob, her tears soaking my hair. After a moment, she pulled back and glanced at the car. Bobby had opened the door and was trying to talk to Dad. But Dad was unconscious.

'Dad?' he asked for the fifth time, before turning to face me with wide eyes. 'What happened? What's wrong with him?'

I didn't know how to answer. Not without remembering things I wanted to forget. Mom rushed to his side and tried to get some reaction out of Dad.

'Let me see him,' Karen said. Mom and Bobby stepped back to let her pass. She bent over Dad and pressed two fingers against his throat, checking his pulse. Her brows knitted together.

My heart plummeted. Please, let him be alright. He can't die. Not now. Not after we'd found him.

'Joshua, Geoffrey, help me carry him into the cottage. I need to take care of his leg,' Karen ordered.

'I can help, too,' Bobby said eagerly. His eyes were glassy and red. He must have been crying.

Karen nodded, waving him closer.

Bobby's clothes were as ill-fitting as Mom's, but then he hadn't worn clothes that fitted him since his last growth spurt. His own trousers had barely reached his calves and had been too tight. These looked like they belonged to a grown man. Tyler, probably. The shirt was black with a silver dagger on the chest, and the jeans were too long, with several fringed holes along the legs. They'd been rolled up, so he wouldn't step on the hems.

I tried to ignore the ache of my muscles and the pain in my feet. Flames seemed to lick at my soles. The stitches must have burst open.

Karen and Bobby grabbed Dad's legs, Geoffrey took his shoulders and head, and Joshua supported his waist. Dad hung limply in their grasp, his mouth slack. He didn't look well. Not at all. His hair and clothes were soaked with sweat, his skin sickly pale.

Mom walked beside them as they carried Dad into one of the small cottages, tears running down her face.

'Well done.' Larry put his hand on my shoulder, squeezing gently.

I gave him a weak smile. 'He doesn't look good. I'm scared that he won't make it.' I pressed my lips together to stop myself from crying. Be strong, I reminded myself.

Larry gave me a look of understanding, his eyes kind. 'Karen is a good nurse. She'll help him. I looked much worse when I arrived in Safe-haven. The muscles in my leg couldn't be mended, but I survived.'

Larry was only a couple of centimetres taller than me, so I didn't have to crane my neck to look him in the eyes. 'Are you immune to the rabies?' I asked.

He seemed to consider my question for a moment. 'I must be. The wound on my leg was the result of a bite from a Weeper. If I weren't immune to the virus, I'd have turned into a beast by now, wouldn't I?'

'Probably,' I said. 'How did you and Karen manage to escape them?'

'I was too badly injured to do much and my memory of the events is a bit hazy. Karen saved us. She shot a few of them, hot-wired a car and drove us here. She's an amazing woman.' He smiled.

'So you knew about Safe-haven?'

He nodded. 'Yes. Karen and I had been in touch with Geoffrey while we were still in our bunker. When we ran out of food, we decided to come here. Unfortunately, we noticed the Weepers in our front garden too late.'

We'd been lucky. I wasn't sure if Dad and I would have survived if a group of Weepers had attacked us right in front of our home. Joshua wouldn't have been there to help us.

Larry clasped his hands behind his back and raised his head to stare at the cloudy sky. 'Karen will do everything in her power. What happens after that is not up to us.' He patted my shoulder. 'Maybe you should try to rest a bit.'

I shook my head. 'I'll check on my dad.'

He turned around and limped towards Rachel, who stood in front of the house, looking lost. I'd totally forgotten about her.

'You must be hungry and probably want to take a shower. Come on, I'll show you around your new home,' Larry told her.

Rachel glanced at me. I gave her an encouraging smile and nodded towards Larry. She followed him and the front door fell shut behind them.

I leaned against the car. So much had happened today. The Weepers. And the poor man who'd fallen from the fire ladder. I couldn't stop thinking about how he'd lain on the concrete, sprawled out, wide-eyed, lifeless. I wished I could banish the memories from my head, forget everything that had happened. I couldn't check on Dad like this. A crying daughter wouldn't help him.

'Hey.'

Joshua's voice made me jump. I hadn't even heard him approach. He stood in front of me, his forehead creased in worry. He reached out, hesitated a few centimetres from my cheek and then cupped it. My skin grew warm under his touch and I leaned into his hand. So strong. So good.

'You alright?' he asked quietly, his blue eyes searching mine. They were so light, like a cloudless sky. I tried to smile, but instead my face crumpled. I shook my head. I wasn't alright. Not at all. These last two days had been hell. Everything I'd seen, all the fear—and so many deaths. I couldn't hold back the tears any more. I hated being so weak, hated

166

breaking down. I needed to be strong for my family. I *wanted* to be strong for them.

'I'm fine,' I choked out, followed by a sob. It wasn't very convincing, of course. I was so pathetic.

Joshua shook his head. 'You don't seem fine.' He leaned against the car, wrapped an arm around my shoulder and pulled me to him. He rubbed my arm gently, staring off into the hills.

'You're right. I'm not fine,' I admitted with a weak laugh.

We stayed like this for a moment, but thoughts of Dad flashed in my mind. The fever, the infection, his paleness.

'I'm worried about my father,' I got out.

'Karen is taking care of him. She'll make sure he gets better.' Joshua caressed my arms, his fingers gentle, our bodies leaning against each other. His warmth and scent were comforting.

'But she won't be able to help him if he's got rabies. Nobody will be able to help him then.'

Joshua's hand tightened briefly on my arm, before he ran it up and down again. 'If he hasn't been bitten by one of them, the chances are slim that he's infected.' His voice was flat. 'Why don't you go in there and ask Karen.' He nodded towards the small cottage.

'Okay.' I lifted my head from his chest. My eyes lingered on his face. His gaze was steady as he looked at me.

I stood on my tiptoes, took a deep breath. I'd fought Weepers. I could do this. I pressed a soft kiss against his cheek. My face grew hot, but I ignored it. 'Thank you for helping me.'

I hurried towards the small cottage and stole a glance over my shoulder. Joshua was staring at me

167

with a look of surprise.

I entered the cottage, a fluttering in my stomach. The hall was narrow and dust hung in the air. Voices were coming from the room to my right. It looked like an improvised infirmary. There was a bed in the centre and a table next to it, with all kinds of medical equipment. The floor was wooden and the walls were an odd yellow. Better than the sterile white walls of the bunker beneath my home.

Geoffrey stood beside me, his arms crossed in front of his chest. His hair hung limply around his face. The shadows beneath his eyes and the deep creases around them made him look old. He spoke when he noticed my gaze on him.

'We prepared this room because we didn't know how many people you'd bring to Safe-haven and what condition they'd be in. It's better than keeping them in the house. If they're infected…'

He trailed off, glancing at Bobby and my mother. How much had they been told?

Mom bent over Dad's head, smoothing his clammy hair. Her lips were moving fast, whispering words of encouragement. She'd stopped crying and looked composed. She seemed stronger than I'd seen her in a long time.

Bobby stood next to the bed and stared down at our motionless father with a look of despair. His jaw was set tight. I could tell he was fighting tears.

I approached the bed, scared of what I would see. Karen stopped what she was doing and glanced up from Dad's leg. The gash in his thigh was long and deep. Even the muscles and tendons were visible. The area around the wound was red and the skin was swollen. She gave me a fleeting smile before she returned her attention to her patient and began

168

cleaning the wound with a swab.

'Can I help?' I asked, though the sight of the gash made me sick. I'd seen worse over the last few days, but the fact that it was Dad's wound made the sight twice as bad.

Karen shook her head. She poked against a part of the wound, and pus oozed out. My stomach tightened. Bobby retched, but he remained where he was. Karen wiped the pus off and rinsed the wound with water. She shook her head with a sigh. 'It shouldn't be inflamed like this.' She looked at Geoffrey. 'There are antibiotics in the cupboard. They've probably expired, but maybe they'll help.'

'Do you think the fever is caused by an infection?' I asked. Mom glanced up from Dad's face, her nervous gaze focused on Karen.

'The infected wound might be the reason,' Karen replied. 'But only time will tell.'

Mom seemed satisfied with the answer and continued talking to Dad, but I'd noticed the caution in Karen's tone.

I leaned down, bringing my face closer to hers. 'When can you be sure that his symptoms aren't signs of rabies?'

Karen began stitching up the wound. 'It isn't a bite wound. I haven't found any on his body yet. Bite wounds are the main cause of a rabies infection. Your father is weak from malnutrition. His body is probably just reacting badly to the injury.'

'How long until we can be *sure* though?' My tone was sharper than I'd intended.

Karen's hand was steady as she continued stitching. 'I don't know exactly. Days, maybe a few weeks.'

A few weeks?

'Here.' Geoffrey handed a small bottle to Karen.

169

She thanked him and began to prepare a drip. 'He needs fluids. It'll strengthen his body and help him fight this,' she explained as she put Dad on the IV.

'Where did you get the medical equipment?' The liquid dripped down the small tube and into Dad's arm. He looked so thin and breakable.

'Joshua searched the local hospitals for anything we could use. I made a list for him and he brought the things that were transportable.' She finished the stitches and started bandaging the leg.

Dad let out a low moan and squirmed on the bed. Mom's head shot up and she looked at us, wide-eyed. I wanted to tell her it would be alright, but the words stuck in my throat.

'He should wake soon. The IV will help,' Karen said. She patted my arm gently before she pulled a chair closer to the bed and sat down.

'You don't need me any more. I'll see what the other arrival can tell me.' Geoffrey dipped an imaginary hat before exiting the room. The door fell shut behind him without a sound.

Mom sank down beside Dad on the bed and rested her head beside his. All their fights in the bunker were meaningless now. I stifled a yawn. My foot burned fiercely, the back of my head throbbed and my ankle hurt like hell. At least now that Dad was safe, I could rest them.

'Karen?' I said.

She glanced at me.

'I think the stitches on my foot might have burst open, and one of the Weepers got its claws on my ankle.'

'What!' Mom exclaimed, sitting up straight with a look of horror, her blonde hair hanging limply over her shoulders.

'I'll take a look at it.' Karen rose from the chair. She patted it, indicating that I should take her seat.

I sank down and pulled off my shoes and socks. Karen grasped my left foot first. Claw marks were visible around my ankle. The skin was an angry red, but it had stopped bleeding. She turned my foot to the side and inspected the wound closely.

'It isn't too bad. The claws haven't dug that deep.' She grabbed a swab from the table and dabbed it in a small bowl. My wound burned like crazy as she cleaned it. I pressed my lips together to keep from making a noise.

'Will Sherry get rabies now?' Bobby asked from his spot next to Dad's bed.

I froze. My chest tightened. I hadn't even thought about that. Mom looked like she was close to having an asthma attack.

Karen shook her head. 'No. Usually a bite wound is necessary. I'll clean this and then it should be alright.'

I slumped against the backrest. She bandaged my ankle and checked on my other foot, clucking her tongue in dismay. 'You strained it too much. It needs new stitches.'

I stifled a groan. But Karen made fast work of the stitches, and I barely noticed the pain. My eyelids felt like they were made of lead and every muscle in my body ached. I'd never felt so exhausted.

Karen released my foot and patted my leg. 'Bobby, Sherry, why don't you go into the main house and have dinner with the others, then go to bed. You look tired. Your mother and I will keep watch tonight.'

I wanted to protest, but I knew I wouldn't be much help. With a weak nod, I began to pull on my

171

shoes and socks, wincing every time I touched my ankle.

My walk towards the door was an awkward hobble. Bobby came up behind me as I stepped out of the cottage. Outside, I looked at the vineyard and the sun setting in the background. It was beautiful. Bobby followed my gaze. He was as tall as I. He'd grown so much in the last few months. When we'd gone into the shelter more than three years ago, he'd still been quite a bit smaller than me. So much had changed since then.

'Do you think Dad will turn into a Weeper?' he asked, trying to keep a brave face. The quiver in his tone revealed how he really felt.

I turned away from the vineyard and faced him. 'No. I'm sure he'll be alright. Karen said it's probably just the infection.'

'I'm not stupid!' Bobby glared at me. 'She only said that because she didn't want to upset us.'

I kicked some dirt with the tip of my good foot. The urge to reassure him was strong, but it would have been unfair to lie.

'I want to believe her.' I shrugged, feeling helpless.

Bobby looked at me, then nodded, satisfied with my answer. He'd probably expected me to lie. But I knew how it felt to be treated like a stupid child who couldn't handle the truth. I wouldn't do that to him.

He took a deep breath. 'Mia asked about you all the time while you were gone. We didn't tell her what happened. Mom thinks it's better if she doesn't know about the Weepers.'

'Mia wouldn't understand. It would only scare her,' I said. Mom had been right.

Bobby nodded, trying to look all grown-up and collected. 'Tell me about them.'

172

I wanted to forget.

'Tell me about the Weepers,' he pleaded.

I stopped and rested my hand on the front door. 'Some of them look almost normal. They walk upright like we do and their eyes are intelligent. Others walk on all fours and their eyes look empty. They're all terrifying and dangerous. They're murderous beasts.' I shuddered and pushed the door open.

Bobby followed me into the hall, his expression determined. 'I want to hunt them like Joshua does.'

I stiffened. Hadn't he listened to what I'd told him? 'It isn't a game, Bobby. They want to kill us... to eat us. We're their prey. They'd kill you.'

'You don't know that! I'd kill them all!' He crossed his arms in front of his chest, defiance flickering in his eyes. If he intended to look like an adult, he failed miserably.

'Killing other creatures isn't as easy as you think. They were people once.' Joshua's voice came out of the darkness. He was leaning against the door frame of the living room, watching us. His face lay in shadows. He flipped a switch and the lights came on in the hall.

'But you hunt them! I want to kill them like you do!'

'You shouldn't do what I do.' Joshua's voice stayed cool.

Bobby glared at him. 'That's stupid! I can do what I want! You can't tell me what to do!' He stormed up the staircase.

Joshua straightened, stretching his arms above his head, his muscles flexing. 'Let's eat.'

I blew out a long breath. My legs felt too heavy to make them carry me anywhere and my feet hurt. I wanted to go to bed, but I was so hungry.

Joshua took my hand and led me into the kitchen.

Grounded.

One week.

Totally unfair.

Not my fault I got detention. If Brittany hadn't made fun of me, I'd never have gotten in a fight with her.

Almost six.

The movie would start at seven.

I grabbed my cell. The movie was my chance to talk to Alex. He'd be there with his friends. It was the only reason Izzy and I even wanted to see that stupid movie. Tucking my phone in my pocket, I sneaked out of my room.

Getting out of the house wouldn't be a problem. Getting back in without my keys was another matter, and I could hardly ask for them.

Dad always hid the spare key in the cookie jar. A stupid place, considering Bobby and I were addicted to cookies. I climbed on the counter and reached for the jar on the highest shelf.

Pushing the cookies aside, something cool brushed my fingertips. The key. I pulled it out.

The rest would be easy. I jumped off the counter.

And froze.

Dad leaned on the door frame. 'You're grounded for another week, young lady.'

CHAPTER TWELVE

Marie sat at the table and watched the stove, her eyes half-closed. Something was cooking in a big pot. It smelled delicious—basil and tomatoes. My stomach rumbled, demanding food.

Mia and Marie's two-year-old daughter Emma sat beside her on the ground, playing with dolls. I'd never been the doll-playing type of girl, though Mom had tried to turn me into one. I'd preferred building blocks and matchbox cars to Barbie and Ken.

Mia looked up, dropping her dolls when she caught sight of me. She jumped to her feet and dashed towards me. Her little head collided painfully with my stomach as she threw herself at me. I hugged her back, despite wheezing for air.

'You're back! You're back!' she shrieked.

I crouched down to be face-to-face with her. Stroking her hair from her face, I smiled. 'I'm back.'

'How's Daddy? Where is he?' She looked past me, as though Dad was hiding somewhere behind me.

'Mom and Dad are in the house next door. You know how adults can be. They want to have an adult talk.' I rolled my eyes exaggeratedly.

'Oh.' Mia scrunched up her nose, believing my lie, though I was a horrible liar. Emma watched me with wide, curious eyes. Her blonde hair was short and fuzzy and she looked like a little boy—a cute one. I straightened up. Mia clutched my hand, as if she was afraid I'd disappear into thin air. I pulled one of the chairs back and plopped down. My feet felt like they were made of stone. Too heavy to lift from the ground.

Joshua was smiling at me, but something about his eyes seemed off. The smile didn't reach them. I wondered what was going on in his head.

Marie put the huge pot with our dinner onto the table. I propped myself up on my elbows and peeked into the pot. There were tomatoes, red peppers, onions and something that looked like chicken or pork.

I glanced at Marie. 'Is that chicken?'

Joshua replied before she could. 'We've got a few chickens and three cows in the garden behind the house.'

912 days since I'd eaten chicken.

'If you want, I can show you around tomorrow.' Joshua filled his plate with food and glanced up at me.

'S-sure,' I stammered, suddenly thinking about the kiss I'd pressed on his cheek. Marie looked between Joshua and me with a grin. I lowered my face and filled my own plate.

Joshua told Marie about our 'adventures', as he called them, in a murmur, so Emma and Mia wouldn't overhear. The stories were terrifying even for me. How much worse would they be for small kids? I wasn't keen on hearing about the horrors again, but I didn't interrupt. Maybe talking about it helped him.

Mia and Emma seemed to get along well, though they were four years apart. After years with only Bobby and me to play with, Mia was probably glad to have another kid around.

'Has Mia had dinner?' I asked. My plate was almost empty. I felt guilty for not having thought about my little sister before.

Marie gave a nod, followed by a yawn. 'Everyone ate before you showed up. We didn't know when you'd come back, so we didn't wait.' She shook her head and opened her eyes wide to stay awake. 'I need to get some sleep. It's already dark outside.' She picked up her daughter, who protested loudly.

'Goodnight,' I called after them.

Marie waved her hand as she left the room. Mia came up to me and hugged my middle, burying her head against my stomach. Joshua had his head propped on his crossed arms, his eyes closed. We all needed a good dose of sleep, even though I wasn't looking forward to the nightmares.

Mia had instantly fallen asleep and hung awkwardly over my lap. I nudged her. Her eyes opened a bit. 'I can't carry you upstairs.' My injured feet could barely carry my own weight, much less additional baggage. She released her grip on my waist and stood, rubbing her eyes with her small fists. Joshua was fast asleep. His breathing was regular and his expression so peaceful. He looked cute. I realized I wanted to kiss him again.

I felt myself blush. It was strange to be interested in a boy again. Watching his untroubled face another moment, I decided not to wake him. Every minute of sleep without nightmares was precious.

I rose, careful not to make too much noise as I pushed my chair back. Mia latched onto my hand and leaned against me. My absence had made her even clingier.

I led her up the stairs. 'Where did you sleep last night?' I tried to keep my voice down.

'In Mommy's bed, but she's not there. I want to sleep in your bed.' She made big puppy-dog eyes and pouted, making me laugh.

'Okay, but you must sleep in your own bed soon. You're a big girl,' I told her. She nodded her head with a little smile and followed me into my bedroom, where she crawled into my bed.

My skin was sticky with sweat, but I was too tired to take a shower. Mia's warm body snuggled against me and I held her as she relaxed into sleep.

*   *   *

Morning came too quickly. I stared at my reflection in the mirror. I'd showered and brushed my teeth, even run a comb through my hair. I felt better, but I still looked like hell. I was pale and there was a bluish bruise on my temple. It looked bad, but it didn't hurt much, or maybe I was too distracted by the pain in other parts of my body to feel it. My feet were worse and the back of my head wasn't great either. I couldn't stop myself from touching the stitches there. My night had been terrible. I'd even woken Mia with my nightmares. Good thing she didn't know what I'd dreamed about.

I couldn't wait to go and see if Dad was better. Maybe he was awake and I could talk to him.

I checked my reflection again. The clothes that I'd found on the desk in my bedroom that morning fitted well. A simple T-shirt and jeans, nothing fancy. I wished I had something prettier to wear. I guessed I'd have to settle for acceptable.

At least my hair looked shiny. The thought made me laugh. It felt good to worry about such silly things, even for just a few minutes, instead of worrying about Weepers who wanted to eat everyone.

69 days since I'd laughed without guilt.

For a moment I felt like a normal teenager, but the stabbing pain in my right foot brought me back.

Mia was still fast asleep, snuggled against the pillows. The sun had just risen and I didn't want to wake her. I closed the door without a sound and made my way downstairs.

Mom sat at the kitchen table next to Karen and Larry, sipping at a cup of coffee. She glanced up. 'Good morning.'

'Morning.' I sank down on a chair, bracing myself for bad news. 'How's Dad?'

Mom's smile thinned. 'He was awake for a few hours during the night, but he's fallen asleep again. He's looking better.'

'Can I go see him?'

'Maybe later. Geoffrey and Bobby are with him now and they'll call us if he wakes. He needs to rest,' Karen said. She, too, looked exhausted.

'Your grandmother has even paid him a short visit.' Mom took another sip from her coffee. 'It was the first time that she's left your grandpa's side.'

I clapped a hand against my forehead. I'd completely forgotten about Grandma. 'Where is she? I haven't seen her.'

'She's with your grandfather in one of the small outhouses,' Larry said.

I knitted my brows. 'Have you put him in the freezer?'

Larry spat out some coffee, coughing desperately. Karen patted his back, fighting laughter.

Mom sighed. 'No, we didn't put him in the freezer.'

'We don't have one that could fit him.' Larry gave me a sheepish look.

'But isn't he…decaying?' I asked. The thought made my stomach squirm.

181

'Unfortunately, yes.' Karen shrugged. She didn't appear bothered by the fact that a body was rotting in the neighbouring cottage.

Mom set down her cup. 'We'll bury him this morning. He's starting to smell. I don't care what your grandma says. It needs to be done.'

I grabbed a cup and spooned in some instant coffee. I'd never drunk coffee before—the smell repulsed me—but now was a good time to start. I took a gulp of the scalding liquid, wincing at the bitter taste, as I tried not to think about dead bodies.

'Is Mia still asleep?' Mom asked, watching her own coffee swirl around as she tilted her cup.

'Yes, she was pretty tired.'

'Good. Then we should do it now, so she won't notice anything.'

'Now?' I asked with a frown. 'Someone needs to dig a grave first.' My feet weren't in favour of volunteering for the task.

Mom got up. 'Tyler and Geoffrey did that a few hours ago.'

'I'll get the others then,' Larry said. My eyes followed him as he limped out of the kitchen.

*   *   *

Karen, Mom and I walked over to the small cottage where Grandma kept watch over Grandpa's body. I put a hand over my nose and tried to breathe through my mouth. I was sure I'd throw up the coffee, but I got myself under control.

Karen didn't react. Maybe you got used to smells like that when you'd been working as a nurse for years. I didn't think I ever could. I followed Mom and Karen into the back of the cottage, where the room was sparsely furnished with a bed and a rocking chair.

Grandma sat on the chair, staring at the ground where Grandpa's body lay. The months in the freezer and the time in this room had left their mark. Most of his body was wrapped up in the blanket, but someone had freed his head. Probably Grandma.

I had to look away. My lips pressed together and I leaned against the door frame. I wouldn't set a foot into the room. Any step closer to the stench and even my willpower wouldn't keep me from throwing up.

Grandma looked up from the ground, her expression empty.

'It's time to bury Edgar,' Mom said gently. Grandma stared at her blankly as if she had no idea what that meant. Hopefully, I wouldn't have to help carry Grandpa's body. That would end in a mess.

Someone tapped me on the arm. I spun around. Joshua's face was pulled into a grimace because of the stench.

'We've come to bring your grandfather outside,' he said through gritted teeth, breathing through his mouth.

We? I peeked behind him and was surprised to see Tyler. I hadn't seen him since that first morning. He normally kept to himself. Maybe he was just shy.

I stepped back so the boys could enter the room. They were carrying a stretcher and heaved the body on it. I moved into the hall to give them more room while they carried Grandpa out of the house. Grandma, Mom, Karen and I followed a few steps behind. We walked into a vast garden overlooking the vineyard. Only the stone wall with its ivy tendrils

183

obstructed the view.

Bobby and Larry had gathered next to a small gate, which they opened for Tyler and Joshua. After a few minutes, we came to a meadow. A huge oak tree towered above a dozen small wooden crosses. Names were carved into a few of them, the rest were blank.

A graveyard.

My stomach churned when I thought about the people who'd died at Safe-haven. What if Dad ended up like them?

We gathered around a hole in the ground. The three cows that Joshua had mentioned were grazing in the background. They raised their heads to gaze at our little gathering in mild interest, chewing unhurriedly. It was an odd sight for a funeral. None of us were dressed appropriately either, but when every day was a struggle for survival, you couldn't worry about proper clothes. Joshua had been right—manners didn't matter any more.

Marie and Geoffrey were missing because someone needed to keep watch over Dad, Mia and Emma.

Dad would be upset that he'd missed Grandpa's funeral. *If he survives.*

I forced those thoughts out of my head. Dad wouldn't share Grandpa's fate. *He*'d make it.

A prickling on my neck, as if someone or something was watching us, sent a shiver down my back. The vineyard looked like it always did, but it was easy to hide between the overgrown vines. Had Weepers followed us? Or was it something else?

I looked away from the vine leaves swaying in the wind and the dark clouds throwing shadows on them.

184

Tyler and Joshua awkwardly lowered Grandpa's body into the grave, careful not to drop him. He didn't even get a coffin. Mom wrapped her arms around Grandma when they began to cover the body with soil. Larry spoke a few words, but I barely listened. I stared at the grave, wondering why I wasn't crying. I'd never been to a funeral before, but it was expected for family members to cry.

I wasn't even particularly sad. So many months had passed since Grandpa had died and I'd said goodbye to him when Dad had put him in the freezer. Back then I'd cried, but now I just felt empty. It worried me. Maybe I was becoming numb.

My gaze swept over the others. Nobody was crying, not even Grandma.

Tyler put the last scoop of soil on the grave before stepping back. Larry's words had long ended and an odd silence followed. The wind picked up, tousling my hair and making me shiver. My T-shirt wasn't enough to protect me. Slowly, everyone walked away from the grave until only my family was left. Then Mom led Grandma back to the house and Bobby followed. As I lingered for a moment, a familiar buzzing drew my eyes to the sky, and I glimpsed a dot growing smaller in the distance. Again? I was really starting to feel like it was following me. What the heck was it?

No answers came to me as I stood there, my gaze wandering over the surrounding slopes, overgrown with vines. Suddenly there was a flash in the distance, as if something had moved. Weepers? Fear gripped my throat.

I squinted my eyes, trying to get a better look. But there was nothing. First the black dot, now this. Maybe I was beginning to imagine things. This wasn't good. Not good at all.

I turned, then started when I noticed Joshua sitting on the wall, watching me. Rubbing my arms to warm myself, I went to him. If he hadn't seen anything move, then there definitely hadn't been anything.

He pushed himself off the wall and landed on his feet with ease—I'd have broken my legs doing that.

Joshua walked up to me, hands in his pockets and his blond hair in disarray. He stopped in front of me, his eyes flitting over to the fresh grave.

'I wish I could have buried my mother.'

I blinked up at him, not sure what to say. 'What happened to her?'

They'd totally ruined my hair.

Ugh.

I glared at my reflection. Teary eyes. Red nose. And what they called a haircut. I looked like a freak. A total mess. Layered cut—the heck it was.

I couldn't go to school like this. What if Brittany saw me? She and her hyenas would taunt me for weeks. And Alex…

I blew my nose.

'Rudolph the red-nosed reindeer had a very shiny nose…'

I whirled around. Bobby stood in the doorway, grinning. He always sang that song to tease me when my nose was red from crying.

'Rudolph the—'

I lunged at him, but the little rat was fast. He dashed down the hall and into his room. The door closed in front of my face. I hammered against it while he sang the stupid song. Over and over and over again.

'Shut up!' The wood vibrated under my fists. 'Bobby, I swear I'll kill you if you don't stop!'

He didn't stop. His voice grew louder.

I sank to the ground. He'd have to leave his room sometime. And I'd be there to kick his ass.

CHAPTER THIRTEEN

Joshua took a step closer and clasped my hand, interlinking our fingers. He led me to an old wooden bench beside the wall and pulled me down with him. I listened to the howling wind while Joshua tried to find words. I didn't want to pressure him.

'We were still in the bunker. We'd been there over a year and the mood was getting worse every day.' He swallowed. 'My sister Zoe was hungry and there was a group of men in the bunker who kept an eye on the food. Zoe walked up to them. Maybe she told them that she was hungry. I don't know.'

I waited for him to go on. He was obviously struggling with the memories of that day. His grasp on my hand tightened.

'The leader of the group pushed her away and she fell down. When Mom saw it, she ran towards them. She said something to the man, and then he and his friends began to hit and kick her. I tried to stop them, but I was only fifteen and there were so many of them. Nobody came to help. Everyone was hungry and didn't want to get into trouble. When the men had finally calmed down, I was covered with bruises, but my mother was unconscious.'

A tear rolled down his cheek.

'She never woke up. Two days later she was dead.' He cleared his throat and ran a hand over his eyes. When he looked at me, his expression was collected, but his eyes couldn't hide his pain.

'What happened to…to her body?' I asked gently.

Joshua's face darkened, anger replacing the sadness. 'The men who killed her took her out of the

189

bunker. They didn't let me go with them and they never told me where they'd put her.' His voice became oddly calm. 'I would've searched for her body, but I had to take care of Zoe. She was only eight.'

Tears made my vision blurry.

'The murderers got what they deserved. A group of Weepers attacked them after everyone had left the bunker. I saw it, but I didn't try to help them, even though I had a gun. I'd stolen it from them just before.'

His voice turned cold. Vicious. He closed his eyes and sucked in a deep breath. What had happened to his mother was horrible, and I had a feeling that the story about his sister's death was just as bad. Maybe talking about it after all this time would help.

'What about your sister, Zoe?'

'I tried to protect her. There was no one left who could except for me. It was just the two of us. The other survivors were busy taking care of themselves. I wanted to be a good big brother for her, but when the Weepers attacked the place where we spent the night, everyone panicked. I lost her in the chaos. I tried to find her. But there were so many people. And then I saw one of the Weepers grab her.'

My chest tightened as he opened up to me. 'The Weeper you tried to chase at the harbour?'

Joshua gave a nod. 'I wanted to get to her, help her, but suddenly they were gone. Afterwards, when the Weepers had left, I looked for her, but I only found one of her shoes. There was blood on it.' He shuddered before taking a deep breath and opening his eyes. 'I thought she was dead. Then, on a hunt, I saw her. She was one of them. A Weeper.'

'Are you sure it was her?'

I couldn't imagine seeing Mia as a Weeper—her blue eyes milky, her face twisted with a snarl. I thought about Dad. Was he already on his way to becoming one of them?

I'd never let that happen.

'It was her, there's no doubt.'

'At least she's alive.'

Joshua blanched. 'Do you think? I think death is better than *that*.'

Maybe he was right.

'What did you do?'

'Nothing. I couldn't help her and I couldn't kill her. I should have.'

I wanted to hug him but I wasn't sure if he'd want me to. 'No, she's still your sister.'

He looked so miserable. '*God,* I miss her. I want her back.'

'I'm sorry,' I whispered.

Joshua was silent for a long while, trying to compose himself. I wished I could console him. After Mom and Dad had fought in the bunker, consoling them had been easy. I'd just told them that they would make up and everything would be okay. But nothing could bring Joshua his mother and sister back, or erase the horrible memories. I felt helpless.

'I don't like to think about it. It's bad enough that I dream about it,' he said, opening his eyes. He tilted his head to the side, his gaze becoming intense. Fidgeting with my feet, I bit my lip and put my free hand in my pocket.

'Do you want me to show you around now? You probably don't want to after everything...' He made a gesture at the freshly dug grave and stared at the ground.

It took me a moment to understand what he meant. 'No, no. I think we both need a distraction.'

He grinned. Some of the darkness disappeared from his eyes. 'Okay then, let's go.'

There it was again: his sudden shift of mood. He wanted to forget. I was beginning to understand that. It'd been only a few days since I'd left the bunker and there were already things I didn't want to be reminded of. Ever.

'I just need to find a sweater or a jacket. It's pretty cold,' I told him with a wave at my thin T-shirt as I got up from the bench. I could have sworn his gaze lingered on my chest longer than necessary.

Joshua slipped out of his hoodie and held it out to me. He was only wearing a T-shirt beneath it himself, showing his muscled chest and arms. I frowned at the offered hoodie.

'Take it,' he urged.

I shook my head. 'You'll freeze.'

'No, I won't. Here, take it.'

I took the hoodie with a mumbled thanks and pulled it on over my T-shirt. It was still warm from his body and smelled of him. Like an autumn forest. I smiled at him shyly. He reached for my hand and clasped it in his again. It felt right. Perfect.

We strolled towards the small gate and walked through it into the garden. 'Apple trees.' He pointed at a group of trees, then led me the other way. 'And there's the vegetable patch. Marie takes care of it. She's very protective of her vegetables, so we'd better stay away.'

I tried to pay attention as he went on about the different vegetables, but his closeness was distracting. A few chickens pecked the ground, searching for food in the grass. The rooster strutted around them, his red comb wobbling with every step. He kept an eye on me, suspicious. Maybe he thought I'd kidnap his hens. His sudden crow made me jump and clutch at Joshua's arm.

He snickered. 'You're jumpy.'

I scowled at him. 'I didn't expect the crow. I thought roosters only crow at sunrise.'

'Our rooster crows whenever he feels like it. He's cocky like that.' A grin crept over his face.

I bumped my shoulder against his. 'Like you.' I smiled, letting my gaze wander over the surrounding vineyard. 'I'd really like to take a walk through the vineyard, if that's okay?' I peeked up at Joshua. The wind kept blowing his blond hair into his face.

He stared into the distance.

'Is it too dangerous?' I asked.

He lifted his T-shirt, revealing a gun in his waistband—and a slash of tanned, taut stomach. The sight of the gun should have calmed me, but it didn't. Instead, I suddenly felt sick at the thought of living in a world where we had to carry guns in our own garden. I sighed.

'When do you think all this will end?' I said. 'What happens next?'

Joshua shook his head. 'We can't keep on living like this for ever. Searching for food and gas, hunting Weepers, it all seems so pointless after a while. There must be more we can do, other places we can explore.'

'You mean, leave Safe-haven?'

'No, not really. For a while maybe, to find out more about the rest of the country.'

'Maybe we could try to contact other survivors again.'

'Yeah. That would be an option, *if* we could reach

193

them.' He paused. 'Don't you think it's strange that the radios suddenly stopped working?'

'What do you mean?' I hadn't thought about the radios before now.

'Our radio worked, we could communicate with other safe havens, and then suddenly we couldn't. You said your radio worked and then, poof, suddenly it didn't. It's kind of strange. It's as if someone doesn't want us to communicate.'

'But who? There's nobody around.' Apparently, I wasn't the only one becoming paranoid.

He looked up and something in his eyes made me pause. 'I've never told anyone about this, but a few weeks ago I noticed something strange during a hunt.'

My heart swelled with pride and something else I couldn't identify—he trusted me. I moved closer, my body prickling with curiosity. 'What did you notice?'

'Geoffrey had asked me to look for radios, because ours had stopped working. He wanted to get back in contact with the other safe havens. So I went to a hardware store that I knew still had radios, but they were all gone. A dozen radios, disappeared. As if they'd vanished into thin air.'

'Gone?'

'Yes. It was like someone had taken them.'

'Maybe it was other survivors?' But there didn't seem to be many of us left.

'Maybe.' Joshua's tone made it clear that he didn't believe it. 'But when I left the store, I saw something in the sky. It was moving.'

'A black dot,' I said. A feeling of unease swelled in my stomach.

'Yes.' Joshua's eyes searched my face. 'You've

194

seen it too?'

'A few times, but I didn't know what it was.' So it wasn't my imagination.

Joshua's expression became distant.

I touched his arm. He blinked, then his eyes focused on me. 'What do you think it is?' I asked.

'I'm not sure.' The look on his face told me he had an idea but wasn't ready to share it with me yet. His trust had a limit. 'Let's not think about it now,' he said abruptly, taking my hand. It was like he had suddenly shut himself off.

He led me back to the main building and across the courtyard towards the vineyards. Even with the cloudy sky, the sight was beautiful. It was easy to forget the horrors of this new world while looking at the beauty surrounding us. We strolled through one of the rows between the vines. The silence was calming, not unsettling like the one that hung over downtown.

Joshua slowed down as we turned back in the direction of the house. I glanced up at him.

He was looking at me with a strange expression, one I'd never seen on his face. I was unable to look away. Slowly, he leaned down, bringing his face closer to mine.

I was frozen to the spot.

He was going to kiss me.

My heart threatened to burst through my ribcage. Maybe I should have made it easier for him and stood on my tiptoes, or lifted my face towards his, but all rational thought had left my mind. He was so close.

His warm breath fanned over my skin and my eyes shut.

There was a rustling a few rows from us. My eyes

195

shot open. We froze, stared at each other and pulled apart. My skin tingled with anxiety. There was something in the vineyard with us. Joshua grabbed his gun, his face and posture alert. Without warning, he pulled me behind him, shielding me.

You don't have a gun, do you? You left it on your nightstand, a voice in my head taunted. I was an idiot.

More rustling made me tense up. I felt Joshua do the same. It came closer and closer. Joshua aimed his gun in that direction. Something shot out from behind the vine. A startled cry escaped my lips and I prepared to run.

Joshua shot but missed.

An alarmed chicken dashed across the row, cackling loudly. Just a chicken. Joshua and I looked at each other and burst out laughing. He lowered his gun.

'Paranoia!' he said with a grin, but I didn't miss the lingering apprehension in his eyes. My heart was still pounding in my chest.

'Come on, let's get back to the house.'

The incident with the chicken had been a good reminder: we were never safe.

I spread my arms, fingers brushing the moist grass blades.

A soft drizzle chilled the night. My lungs filled with air. Refreshing and cool.

A full moon. Small water droplets on the grass glittered in the silver light. It illuminated our garden. Everyone was asleep, the light in the neighbouring houses extinguished.

'Sometimes I wonder what our life will be like in ten years,' Izzy whispered.

'I don't know. I hope I'll work as a vet. That's what I'd like to do.'

'Hmm. Sounds like a plan.' She yawned. 'I've got no clue what I want.'

'Twenty-two, that's kind of old, isn't it?'

'Yeah. I bet you'll be married to Alex and have a bunch of kids.'

'You're stupid.'

She grinned, but it faded. 'Do you think we'll still be best friends?'

'Of course. Best friends for ever.'

'Best friends for ever.'

CHAPTER FOURTEEN

I buried my face in the soft pillow, trying to return to sleep. A nightmare must have woken me. At least I hadn't disturbed Mia. She was snuggled against my body, her face resting against my chest. My eyes felt heavy. It wouldn't take long to fall back to sleep.

Tick-tick.

I turned my face away from the pillow and opened my eyes.

Tick-tick.

What was that noise?

I held my breath and listened.

Tick-tick.

It sounded like someone—or something—was tapping their fingernails against the window.

I swallowed. The thud-thud of my pulse filled my ears, like a bassline turned up high. I shifted on the bed, careful not to wake Mia, and tried to get a look at the window. Moonlight streamed into the room and illuminated the floor. A moving shadow parted the beam of light. My heartbeat quickened and my mouth went dry. Something was in front of the window and tapping against the glass.

I didn't need to see it to know it was a Weeper. The window wouldn't stop it for long. With its strength, bursting through the glass wouldn't be a problem. I had to protect Mia. I wouldn't let *anything* hurt her.

Where was my gun?

I inched closer to the edge of the bed and the nightstand where the gun lay. Mia stirred, making me freeze.

'Sherry, wha's up?' Her voice was muffled by my chest and her hold on me tightened.

The tapping got louder, more insistent. I needed to get out of bed. My hand moved closer to the gun—centimetre by centimetre. Mia shifted and looked at me, then her eyes grew wide. 'Tapping,' she mouthed. I put my finger against my lips.

A scream resounded in the silence, setting my teeth on edge.

Mom. That was Mom's voice!

What if she was alone in the small cottage with Dad?

I jumped out of the bed and grabbed my gun from the nightstand. My eyes settled on the Weeper balancing on the window sill of my room. Its moist eyes stared right at me, its inhuman face twisted into an ugly grimace, showing off several sharp teeth. I shot twice, ignoring Mia's scream. The Weeper pushed itself off the ledge before a bullet could hit it.

I rushed towards the broken window and shot a few more times at the Weeper fleeing across the courtyard. I couldn't let it get Mom or Dad or anyone else. I had to stop it. The third shot brought it down. It lay unmoving on the ground.

Screams rang out in the house and more were coming from the cottage. The windows were dark but I could make out a commotion.

My eyes landed on Mia, who sat on the bed, shaking, tears streaming down her pale face.

I needed to help Mom, but I couldn't leave my sister alone.

Shots sounded in the house. Roars and more screams followed. Panic swelled in me. I grabbed Mia and pressed her against my chest. She wound her legs around my waist and clung to me. I tiptoed towards the door and opened it a crack, gun at the ready.

I crept into the hall. Mia's hands clutched at me and their grip tightened with every gunshot. It sounded like a war was raging downstairs—and I wasn't there to help. I didn't want to leave Mia alone, but her weight would only hinder me. And that would put us both in danger.

The screaming downstairs got louder. I needed to make a decision. Quick.

I prised Mia's arms from my neck and lowered her to the ground. She clung to me, her eyes wide and fearful as she gazed up at me.

'Mia, I need to help downstairs. Stay here. I'll be back soon.'

She wound her arms around my waist and shook her head frantically. 'No. Don't leave me alone!' Her sobbing tore at my heart, but she was safer here than with me downstairs.

I loosened her grip and opened the door of the linen closet. I pushed the heaps of towels and linen aside, so Mia could walk in. 'Listen, Mia. I promise I'll be back very soon. Just wait here. Be quiet and don't move.'

She sank down to the ground and leaned against the wall, giving a small nod. I positioned the heap of towels in front of her and closed the door, before rushing towards the staircase. I froze halfway down the landing.

A Weeper cowered on the last step. Its yellowish eyes settled on me, tears pouring out of them, and it snarled, spit dripping from its lips. I wanted to run and hide, but I didn't.

It pushed up from the step and propelled itself

towards me. My heart pounding in my chest, I raised the gun and shot.

A bullet cut through its neck, blood flying everywhere, and the Weeper landed with a thud on the stairs below me. It twitched as if hit by electric shocks.

I caught my breath and moved closer. My body trembled when I leaned over to check if it was really dead. The way its skull was broken left me in no doubt. Shreds of skin covered the stairs.

Swallowing down my sickness, I stepped over the corpse and walked towards the commotion in the living room. A dead Weeper lay just in front of the doorway, bleeding all over the flowery carpet.

The house was silent. I glanced to the side and saw Larry and Geoffrey in the living room, armed with guns. Two Weepers lay at their feet. One of them was dead, the other still whimpering. They didn't need my help any more.

Gunshots cracked outside and I whirled around. Without thinking, I stormed towards the front door and ripped it open. The scene outside nearly brought me to my knees.

Several Weepers lay sprawled in the courtyard, the pebbles surrounding them shiny red with blood, and amongst them was a human body. Or what was left of it. Not much. Bile rose in my throat.

I grabbed the door frame to steady myself, my vision swimming. Thunder rumbled over Safe-haven, lightning flashing across the sky. Joshua stepped out of the cottage and came up to me, two guns in his hands. He was only wearing pyjama bottoms, his chest bare. Sweat glistened on his skin. He'd been with Mom and Dad.

'You alright?' he asked, his eyes sweeping over

me. It started pouring down on us, raindrops lashing against my face.

I gave a weak nod. 'Mom? Dad?' My voice quivered.

'They're okay.'

I swallowed down a bitter taste and nodded towards the body.

Joshua followed my gaze and his expression softened. He cupped my cheeks. 'I'm sorry. I was too late. Your grandma ran out of the house to get to your grandfather's grave before we could stop her. The Weepers killed her instantly.'

Grandma was dead. Killed by Weepers. If there was anyone who wasn't scared of death, then it was her.

Karen appeared next to us. She'd also come from the infirmary cottage. 'Any injuries?'

I shook my head.

'Larry? Geoffrey?' she called out, and the two came up behind me.

'We're fine,' Larry assured his wife. 'Tyler and Rachel are with Emma and Marie in their room on the upper floor.'

'Where's Bobby?' I looked around, the familiar tremor coming over my body.

'I'm here!' He leaned out of the window of the small cottage and Mom stood behind him.

My heartbeat calmed. We'd survived. Not all of us, I reminded myself. Grandma was gone. But it could have ended worse. So much worse. It was a miracle that more of us hadn't been killed.

'That's the first time they've ever attacked,' Geoffrey said with a puzzled look.

Joshua's expression darkened. 'It won't be the last time.'

Safe-haven wasn't safe any more. That too had been taken from us.

'Where's Mia?' Karen asked.

'Upstairs. I thought she'd be safer there.'

Joshua's face changed. 'Alone?'

'Yes.'

He ran past me without another word. I followed him, stumbling in my haste to keep up.

'Joshua?' I screamed.

He took two steps at once, pointing his guns ahead. Footsteps rang out behind me, but I didn't check who it was.

I reached the first floor a second after Joshua.

'Where is she?'

I opened the door of the linen closet and pushed the towels aside. 'She's...' I trailed off. She wasn't there. I ran into our bedroom, with its broken window and the shards on the ground. 'Mia?'

Nothing but silence.

Joshua stood beside me, his face paler than I'd ever seen it. 'Not again.' Despair rang in his words.

'Mia?' I called, louder this time. Panic corded up my throat and I began to gasp for breath. Oh God, they'd taken her.

'She's gone?' Karen asked from behind me.

'We'll search for her,' Joshua ordered. He pushed past me and stormed into the corridor. I stumbled towards the wardrobe and ripped it open. Mia wasn't in there.

'Mia?' I cried. Hot tears burned in my eyes and trailed over my cheeks.

My eyes settled on the bed and I fell to my knees to check the space beneath it. She wasn't there either. Please not her. Please.

'I have her!' Joshua's shout went right through

me. I shot up and was out of the room within a second. Please let her be alive.

'Joshua?' I screamed.

'I'm here.'

Bathroom.

I rushed into the room. Joshua stood in the shower and held Mia. She had her arms wrapped around his neck and he pressed his cheek against her hair. His eyes were moist, as if he'd been crying.

My legs shook so much that I thought they'd give way.

'Mia.'

She raised her head and looked at me. I took her from Joshua, though he seemed reluctant to let her go. I held her to me tightly while she wrapped her legs around my waist.

'She was hiding in the shower.'

'Thanks.'

Our gazes seemed glued to each other. There were so many emotions in his eyes, so many things I didn't understand.

Mia stirred and I looked at her.

'Why did you hide in the shower? Why didn't you listen to what I told you?'

Her answer was muffled by my chest. 'I saw one of them.'

'One of them?' I exchanged a look with Joshua and his eyes clouded with worry.

'I saw it through the keyhole.'

They'd gotten upstairs.

A crunch startled me. I stared at the ceiling. Another crunch. Like footsteps above us.

'They're on the roof,' Joshua said, wild determination and hatred flashing across his face. 'Stay here, Sherry.' He was out of the room before I could blink.

No way.

Yet I hesitated, torn between my wish to follow Joshua and my fear of letting go of Mia. What if I wasn't there to protect her from another Weeper in the house?

'I can take care of her. I'll keep her safe,' Karen said, extending her arms. After a second I handed Mia over. It felt like a part of my body was ripped off.

I chased after Joshua and caught up with him at the ladder that led to the attic.

He glared at me. 'Sherry, I mean it. Go back to the others. I don't want you up there.'

'Forget it.' I pushed past him and climbed the ladder. I wouldn't let him fight the Weepers alone. I had to protect my family. And Joshua, even if he didn't want my protection. He cussed as he followed me.

The attic was dark and dusty. Only the moon shining through a small window gave any light. Furniture and paintings covered with blankets filled almost the entire space and the aisles in between were narrow, making it difficult to navigate through them.

The noises on the roof grew louder, as if a Weeper was jumping to gain our attention.

Joshua's steely grip around my arm stopped me. He whirled me around so I faced him. My anger crumbled under the look in his eyes. Fear and worry. 'Sherry. It's too dangerous. I don't want you to get hurt.'

'And I won't leave you alone.'

He must have seen my determination because he reached out and stroked my hair, tucking it behind my ear. His touch felt desperate, as if he expected it could be our last.

A bang filled the attic. My hackles rose, an icy chill shooting through my veins.

Not again. One of them was in here with us.

The trapdoor had fallen shut. I strained my eyes, but the furniture blocked my view of our only escape route. There was scratching, as if someone was pushing a heavy piece of furniture around. God, it was a trap. They were barring the flap, keeping us here. The shuffling came closer.

Joshua grasped my hand and dragged me towards the window. It was open.

'I go first,' Joshua said. He leaned out and checked his surroundings, then he climbed up. I hoisted myself out after him and crouched on the roof. Cold wind and rain lashed against us. Slowly I straightened, my arms outstretched to keep my balance. This side of the roof was deserted. One of them was in the attic, but there was at least one more—the one we'd heard walking around up here. Where was it?

I looked at Joshua, but he was staring at the other side of the roof. With the rain, it was impossible to see that far.

A scratching noise to one side startled me. I whirled around. Nothing. My breathing filled the air, loud and raspy. The clouds parted and revealed the full moon, its beams of silver light making Joshua's hair glow.

'Sherry!'

Joshua's scream set my teeth on edge. I raised my gun and fired at a shadow darting out of the window. Fur brushed my arm and a foot or paw kicked into my stomach. The air rushed out of my lungs and I staggered backwards. My feet slipped on the wet tiles and my body collided with the roof. Hard.

Pain shot through me. Hot and searing. Something was definitely broken. I tumbled down the roof, the sharp edges of the tiles biting into my skin, ripping and tearing. My hands slid over the slippery surface. I tried to hold onto something—anything—to stop my fall. Suddenly my fingers clutched the guttering, though my arms screamed at me to let go. I felt my body dangling like a marionette from the roof. The fall would be deadly—and then I wouldn't be able to help Joshua.

Two Weepers circled him in a wide range. He shot, but missed. Hell, they were fast. I tried to pull myself up, but I barely had enough strength to hold onto the gutter. Something wasn't right with my shoulder. I groaned, spasms seizing my body.

Both Weepers lunged at Joshua. A scream ripped from my throat. 'No!'

Shots rang out. A Weeper dropped to the tiles, unmoving. Relief burst through me, but the other Weeper flung Joshua across the roof. He landed on his back with a sickening crack. His gun slipped from his hand, down the tiles and dropped to the ground. He groped around for his hunting knife, but it was also gone. He was unarmed, against an opponent who was impossible to defeat without weapons. Our eyes met and the apology I saw in them sent a new wave of determination through me. I wouldn't let the Weeper hurt him.

'You ugly beast! I'm here!'

The Weeper glanced over its shoulder at me, hollow eyes full of hunger. It was going to eat me. Its teeth would sink into my skin, its claws would rip me apart. But then I saw something. Joshua's hunting knife lay in the gutter a couple of metres away. I couldn't reach it, not with my loosening grip. But Joshua could. Realization filled his eyes.

'Yes, get me, you stupid beast!' I screamed, hating how my voice rang with fear. The Weeper took a step in my direction, nostrils flaring. Could it smell my panic?

Joshua shot to his feet and slid down the roof. His feet bumped against the gutter, stopping his slide. He grabbed the knife and scrambled to his feet. The look in his eyes scared me.

My fingers loosened. Not much longer and I'd be spattered on the pebbles. Cold sweat and rain covered my forehead and dripped into my eyes. I heard voices beneath me. Frantic and scared. But I didn't look down.

Joshua pounced on the Weeper. Their bodies collided. Growls filled the night. Claws ripping, teeth flashing, spit flying.

Joshua would die. My shoulders and arms screamed at me, but it was nothing, absolutely nothing, in comparison to the thought of losing Joshua. I bit down on my lip so hard I drew blood. My arms burned and my palms were slick from blood and rain. I whimpered, but I pulled until I thought my muscles and tendons would rip. My feet searched for footing, but they slipped.

Joshua.

My toes dug into the rough brick. The pain was fierce. Unimportant. I pushed myself up and managed to get my heel on the gutter. It hurt like hell. Worse. Like razors slicing my shoulders, acid burning my soles, needles boring into my fingers. A tremor went through my arms as I hoisted myself up. For a moment, I lay on the roof, my face pressed to the tiles, wet hair sticking to my skin. My body

209

screamed at me not to move.

I stumbled to my feet, disorientated for an instant, and afraid. So damn afraid of what I would see. Joshua dead, ripped apart, lifeless eyes accusing me.

But the fight was in full swing. The Weeper had forced Joshua to the edge of the roof. One more blow and Joshua would fall.

I wasn't sure how I managed to run on the slippery tiles, but I did, and I threw myself at the Weeper. It was crazy. Dangerous. My fingers grasped for its neck.

The Weeper roared. I'd surprised it. It lashed out but missed. I clung to its back as if I wanted it to give me a piggyback. I wouldn't let go, wouldn't let it hurt Joshua. I wouldn't let it get off the roof to kill my family.

'Sherry, let go!'

My hands loosened, taking strips of skin with them, and I landed on my butt, a stabbing pain shooting up my spine. The hunting knife flashed in Joshua's hand, like lightning. He swung it around, slicing the Weeper's throat. A gurgled roar died in its mouth, blood pumping from the wound, covering its chest. The flow from its eyes worsened and the milky tears mingled with red. It staggered backwards and fell off the roof.

Wind tugged at my hair and pressed against my ears. The Weeper was gone—dead. And we'd survived, had protected our family and friends. For a moment I'd been so sure we'd die, but we lived.

We really lived.

Warm arms enveloped me in a crushing hug. Slowly, I leaned against Joshua's chest. It was sticky with blood. I felt his lips against my ear, whispering or kissing, I couldn't tell. I was still so damn dizzy.

His hands cupped my cheeks. So gentle, and yet so relentless when they killed. He pulled my face up. Blood was streaming from a gash over his right eyebrow, covering his face. Moonlight reflected in his eyes, made them sparkle silver.

His lips moved, but I didn't hear him over the whooshing in my ears. His hands pushed my hair back from my face, caressing and searching for injuries. Blood kept dripping into his right eye. He just blinked it away.

'Are you okay?' I asked.

He smiled as if I should know better than to ask. His lips brushed against mine, his palms warm against my cheeks. Our kiss tasted of blood and tears. Of rain and dirt. Of pain and relief. But more than anything, it was a promise. An oath to never let anything happen to the other.

*   *   *

Neither of us returned to bed, though it was the middle of the night. I didn't think I could fall asleep even if I tried. I wasn't sure if I ever could again. The tapping of fingernails against the window chimed in my head. The brightness of fangs and knives flashed in my mind, the taste of blood lingered on my lips.

Cleaning the house, removing the destroyed furniture and burning the dead Weepers took us the morning and early afternoon, but at least it kept us busy—in body and mind. It stopped me from thinking about Grandma.

But in the evening, the smell of charred flesh hung in the air, burned in my nose and eyes. We buried what was left of Grandma next to Grandpa. Finally they were reunited.

211

Music blared in the background. Some kind of rap.

My foot moved in rhythm with it. I didn't even like the song. The beats went right through me, making my body buzz.

I closed my eyes and tipped the bottle, the rim chilled against my lips. The Coke slipped down my throat, cooling me. Clanking—glass on tiles—brought me back.

Light flashed on the bottle. Spinning. Everyone watched it. Waiting. Excited and nervous.

My eyes followed the tip of the bottle. It slowed.

Don't point at me. Don't point at me.

It stopped. Izzy groaned.

'Truth or Dare?' Brittany asked.

'Dare.'

Brittany would use her chance. Stupid cow.

'You have to kiss someone on the lips.'

Her eyes rested on Eric—'the freak', as he was known. I gave Izzy a sympathetic look.

'Alex. Kiss Alex.' Brittany smirked. Izzy stared at me. I clutched my Coke. Avoided her eyes.

I didn't want to see how they moved into the circle, leaned towards each other and…kissed. I jumped up, Coke bottle smashing on the ground. My feet carried me out, tears blurring my vision. I hated Brittany.

Music blared in the background. Some kind of rap.
My foot moved in rhythm with it. I didn't even like
the song. The beats went right through me, making my
body buzz.

I closed my eyes and tipped the bottle, the rim chilled
against my lips. The Coke dipped down my throat,
cooling me. Crackling—glass on ice—brought me
back.

Light flashed on the bottle. Spinning. Everyone
watched it. Waiting. Excited and nervous.

My eyes followed the tip of the bottle. It slowed.

Don't point at me. Don't point at me.

It stopped. Just missed.

'Truth or Dare?' Brittany asked.

'Dare.'

Brittany would use her chance. Sweet cow.

You have to kiss someone on the lips.

The tip rested on Katie—the geek—as he was
known. I gave her a sympathetic look.

'Her. Kiss this.' Brittany smirked. Katie turned around.

I clutched my Coke. I waited for it to—

I didn't want to see how they moved into the circle,
laughing... with what girl... I gripped up.

Coke burst, smashing on the ground. My feet carried
me away. Brittany, my cousin. Happy Birthday.

CHAPTER FIFTEEN

The chirping of birds and the occasional chirring of a cricket was the only sound around us.

6 days and 4 hours since the Weeper attack.

8,880 minutes—but it felt much longer.

Joshua and I had escaped to the vineyard. It had become the place where we could spend time alone, holding each other and kissing. It was our personal safe haven, though nothing was really safe any more, least of all Safe-haven itself. We could never let our guard down. At least Dad was getting better. Karen told me he was doing fine.

Discussions about abandoning Safe-haven dominated every day and worry kept us awake at night. But where could we go? We'd found a home here and that was something hard to come by in this world. Weepers were everywhere. Should we let them drive us away? We'd end up as nomads, travelling from one place to another, searching for safety that no longer existed.

Joshua's arms around me tightened, bringing our bodies even closer together.

'Sherry! Joshua!' Bobby's shout sounded in the silence.

Joshua pulled back with a groan. I opened my eyes, wanting to strangle my little brother. We had so little time alone—every minute was precious. Mom always made sure there was someone with us. I bet she'd sent Bobby to check on us.

'Sherry! Joshua!' The shouting came closer.

'If we duck down, he won't find us,' Joshua said with a wicked smile. It was an appealing thought.

215

I laughed. 'You don't know Bobby, he won't give up.'

'Sherry!'

'We're here!' I shouted.

'Where?'

I rolled my eyes, causing Joshua's grin to widen. 'Here!'

Bobby appeared in our row, his face alight with excitement. Then his brows furrowed. 'Why are you hugging my sister?'

Joshua and I took a step back from each other and dropped our arms. Joshua handled the situation much better than I could have. 'You wouldn't understand.'

Bobby scowled and opened his mouth, but I held up a hand. 'What do you want?' Annoyance crept into my voice. I couldn't help it. I wasn't sure when Joshua and I would be close to each other again, and Bobby just had to come and ruin the moment.

Bobby blinked at me, then the excitement returned to his face. 'Geoffrey managed to get the radio receiver going. He even managed to make it work over a longer distance. There were voices!'

Joshua and I exchanged looks. Voices? Other survivors?

Bobby whirled around and headed back the way he'd come. Joshua and I ran after him.

I was out of breath by the time we arrived in the living room, where Geoffrey had put Dad's radio receiver on a table.

He looked up when we burst in and smiled proudly. 'It works. I pushed the buttons like I always do and suddenly there were voices, but I lost them before we could exchange information. We just need to wait for the voices to return.' He turned the

216

knobs, but all that came from the radio was a swishing noise.

Then suddenly warped voices rang out, overlaid by the constant hissing. I strained my ears to hear what they were saying.

'Hello?' Geoffrey said into the little microphone, moving the aerial back and forth.

'Geoffrey?' A man asked.

'Yes, it's me. I lost you for a moment.'

'Geoffrey, this is important.' The man sounded hurried and frightened. 'We must warn you. They betrayed us. There's—' The hissing returned with full force, cutting the words off.

Maybe Joshua was right and there was someone who didn't want us to communicate.

Joshua looked as clueless as I felt.

'Who has betrayed us?' I asked as we sank down on the sofa, exchanging panicked looks.

Larry occupied one of the armchairs, leaning forward and watching Geoffrey with rapt attention. 'Yes, what does that even mean?'

Joshua pointed at the speakers. 'Who was that guy anyway?'

Geoffrey worked on the back of the radio with a screwdriver, concentration written across his face. 'Simon. He told me his name is Simon. He lives with others in a safe haven in Arizona. That's all I know.'

I slumped against Joshua, feeling exhausted, and waited for something to happen.

*　　　*　　　*

I awoke with a start and my eyes fluttered open. I must have fallen asleep. My head leaned on Joshua's shoulder. Marie and Emma sat on the ground in

217

front of our feet, talking quietly.

I sat up, blinking away the sleepiness. 'How long have I slept?'

'An hour,' Joshua replied in a drowsy voice. 'But you didn't miss anything. Only swooshing.'

I rose from the sofa and stretched my tired muscles. 'I'll check on my father. If anything happens, call me.'

Joshua nodded, eyes half-closed. Larry was fast asleep in his armchair, snoring with his mouth open. I dragged myself towards the front door. Cold wind whipped against my face when I stepped outside. It woke me up.

I crossed the courtyard with hurried steps. Even with Joshua's sweater on, I was freezing. Where had the heat gone?

I walked into the cottage, where Karen sat on a chair, reading a book. She glanced up briefly and smiled at me before returning her attention to the pages. Mom was perched on the edge of the bed, talking to Dad. My heart leaped—he was finally conscious!

Dad's eyes darted towards me. A weak smile curled his lips.

'Sherry,' he said in a croaky voice. Some colour had returned to his face, but he was still on the drip. I rushed towards him and threw my arms around his neck, hugging him tightly. His touch seemed to burn my skin; his fever still hadn't lessened. He laughed hoarsely and stroked my back. Tears prickled in my eyes. A few brimmed over and ran down my cheeks. I pulled back and wiped off the tears with the sleeve of the hoodie. He was awake and he looked better. I was so happy.

Mom gave me a teary smile while she held Dad's

hand.

'I'm proud of you,' he said.

I stared at him. 'W-why?'

Dad rolled his eyes. 'And I thought you were clever,' he joked in his weak voice. Beads of sweat covered his forehead. I hadn't noticed them a minute ago. The fever, the sweating. Signs of rabies?

'You are very brave, Sherry,' he said in his proud-father voice. But there was no reason for him to be proud of me.

'It was my fault the Weepers captured you. I should've stopped them. I came with you to keep you safe and I failed.' My voice broke at the end.

'Don't be silly, Sherry,' Mom admonished with a shake of her head.

'It wasn't your fault. I had the shotgun and I should have defended us, but I dropped it when one of those beasts jumped in front of me.' Dad shuddered at the thought. He took a deep breath before he continued. 'I thought they'd killed you when they didn't bring you to the harbour. I thought I'd broken the promise I'd given to your mother.' He glanced at Mom with an apologetic look.

I gave them their moment of silent understanding and stared down at my hands. Without Joshua's help the Weepers would have ended my life. I'd never forget it.

'How did you manage to survive? It's a miracle,' Dad said in wonder.

I glanced up and smiled. 'Joshua saved me.'

'You're wearing his hoodie.' Mom searched my face.

I felt myself blush. 'I was cold.' What a lame lie. I just liked the smell of it. Mom and Dad exchanged a look I didn't even bother to analyse.

219

The door was thrown open and banged against the wall, making us all jump. I expected a Weeper to be standing in the doorway, but it was only Joshua who stepped into the room.

Karen scowled at him as she picked up her book, which she'd dropped. 'For God's sake, Joshua, do you want to give us all heart attacks?'

Joshua didn't react. 'There's a helicopter circling over Safe-haven!'

'What?' Karen and I asked at once.

'I heard a noise and suddenly it was there!'

My heart leaped into my throat.

'Come on!' Joshua urged. He ran out of the room as if the devil was chasing him.

I sped after him, my eyes searching the sky. And then I spotted it. A black dot in the sky, growing bigger. Yes, it was coming back. It was the black dot that I'd seen several times. Within seconds it was above us and I saw it was a military helicopter. It was flying so low I could even make out the soldiers sitting in it, their faces covered with black gas masks.

There *were* other people. Military. We were saved!

The other members of Safe-haven gathered around us, waving wildly. 'We're here!' we shouted.

Tyler's eyes grew wide and he started to tremble. Slowly he sank to his knees.

I looked over at Rachel, who was standing next to him, but her eyes were fixed on the helicopter. Behind her, Geoffrey appeared in the doorway of the house and stood frozen in the shadows as he stared at the sky.

'It's not slowing down,' Larry said.

'They have to see us. They're so close! How can they miss us?' Karen stared at the helicopter in shock. 'We're down here!' She jumped up and down.

There had to be a way to make them see us, to attract their attention. 'We need a flare gun!' I said.

Joshua bolted past Geoffrey into the house and returned a few seconds later with a boxy-looking pistol. He raised it over his head, but before he could fire it, Tyler tackled him, sending them both flying to the ground. 'Get off me! Are you crazy?' Joshua yelled. He pushed Tyler off and jumped to his feet. Tyler stayed on his back and covered his eyes with his hands. What was the matter with him?

Joshua pulled the trigger.

A light soared into the sky, sparks of glaring red against greyish-blue. It was impossible to miss. But the helicopter didn't change its direction, nor did it dive. It flew on as if we weren't there, though the soldiers must have seen us.

'Why aren't they rescuing us?' Bobby asked, looking at me as if I knew the answer.

'Hey, you bastards!' Joshua shouted. The helicopter was becoming smaller and smaller, until it was nothing but a black dot on the horizon again.

'Maybe they're just waiting for reinforcements,' Marie guessed, clutching Emma to her body.

Tyler cowered on the ground, his head buried in his knees. His body was shaking now and he was rocking back and forth like he'd really lost it. Rachel was behind him, her eyes wide—whether from shock or fear, I couldn't tell. After a moment, Tyler looked up and our eyes met. I knew instantly that something was horribly wrong.

He croaked out something, but after months of not talking, his mouth wasn't used to forming words. It sounded like, 'They won't save us.'

The others looked at him. Shock and confusion mingled on their faces, but I felt only dread.

221

'What did you say?' Joshua asked.

'They won't save us.' Tyler's voice was deep and rough, but so quiet that I had to strain my ears.

'What do you mean, they won't save us? How do you know? I don't understand, Tyler.' Karen walked up to him and put a hand on his shoulder. He flinched as if she'd hit him. Karen exchanged a look with Larry that made it clear she thought Tyler had lost his mind. But somehow I knew the words coming from his lips weren't the result of madness.

'I was there, on the other side.' He pressed his cheek against his knees, his knuckles turning white from his grip on his legs. He looked lost, and so much younger than he was.

'What other side?' I asked, keeping my voice gentle so it wouldn't upset him.

'The other side of the fence.'

Larry pinched the bridge of his nose, pushing his glasses out of the way. 'Fence. I don't get it. What fence?'

Something in Geoffrey's face changed, as if he feared what was coming.

'There's a fence.' Tyler sucked in a breath. It was obvious that every word was a struggle. 'It keeps us and the Weepers here. It separates...separates us from the rest of the country.' He swallowed. 'There's an entire world beyond the fence. A world where life goes on as if nothing h-has happened.' Tyler was still shaking, as if his own words had scared him even more than the helicopter.

That didn't make sense. How could life go on like it used to? How could anyone live a life in safety while we were fighting for survival every day?

'How do you know this?' I asked.

'After I left the public bunker, me and a few others

222

were travelling through the country, searching for more survivors, when a helicopter appeared above us. They shot at us and a tranquillizer dart hit me. After that, I don't remember much. I must have lost consciousness. When I woke up I was in a laboratory, tied to a table. On the other side. Beyond the fence.'

Part of me wanted to block my ears, so I wouldn't hear any more. The other part wanted to learn as much as possible.

'They were using us as lab rats to test the rabies on. There was so much death.' He closed his eyes as if that would make him forget. But I knew it wouldn't; every memory I wanted so desperately to forget seemed even more vivid once my eyes were closed.

There was a moment of silence. I was frozen, and so were the others. My fingers felt numb and slowly the numbness spread through the rest of my body. I couldn't believe what I was hearing.

It was Mom who spoke first. 'They'd never do that.'

Geoffrey grimaced, an odd expression on his face. 'They would, believe me. I've seen a lot in my time as a scientist. Many things that have made me doubt humankind.'

Karen lowered herself to sit beside Tyler. 'But how did you get out of there? Did they let you go?'

A choked laugh left his lips. 'No, they don't let anybody leave who's been in the laboratory. I managed to escape. For days I hid in abandoned houses, before I discovered the fence. Other captives told me about it, but I never believed it was really true. I found a tunnel. It was in bad shape, but I had no choice.' He shuddered.

'When I came out on this side of the fence, I was

223

sick with fever. I ran and ran and didn't stop, but I don't remember what happened after that. The first thing I remember is waking up here.'

'I'm so sorry, Tyler.' Rachel crouched beside him and wrapped an arm around his shoulders.

I couldn't even imagine what Tyler had gone through. I didn't think I'd have survived if I'd been in his place. No wonder he'd stopped talking.

Larry shook his head. 'But why can't we reach anyone with a cell and why isn't there any television reception? If life is going on as it used to be across the country we would have noticed, wouldn't we?'

I took Joshua's hand, needing his support more than ever. He glanced at me and his eyes showed he believed Tyler.

Tyler ran his fingers through the dirt beside his feet, drawing a long line. The words seemed to flow from him more easily now. 'The government was thorough. They made sure nobody found out about us and we never got over the fence unless they wanted us to. There are minefields, spring guns, cameras.'

Larry nodded, his frown clearing as if a riddle he'd been working on had just been solved. 'So they sealed us off from the rest of the world. It must be as if we don't exist. The government is sending interfering waves. That's why we stopped getting a signal.'

'But the world would never allow it—the rest of America would never allow it,' I said. 'Someone would have stopped the government. Wouldn't they?'

Geoffrey rubbed his temples. 'To the rest of the world, we're probably nothing more than dead or infected beasts. They will have been manipulated by the government into believing that we're no longer human.'

The truth sank in. Nobody would help us. Joshua squeezed my hand gently, steadying me with the gesture. I gave him a faint smile, though I'd rather have cried.

'How come we've never seen helicopters or planes or ships before, if the rest of the world is living their lives as if nothing happened?' he asked.

'This is a restricted area. It's prohibited to fly over or set foot in it. They labelled it "contaminated wasteland". I heard them talk about it while I was in the lab,' Tyler whispered, his legs pulled against his chest.

Contaminated wasteland. That's what they called my home.

'Why haven't other survivors seen the fence?' Joshua asked.

'Helicopters are patrolling the fence area. If they catch people nearby, they take them away to the lab. That's what happened to me,' Tyler said.

Geoffrey closed his eyes and ran a hand down his face—he looked grey. And that's when I realized how little he'd said. And suddenly it was obvious.

'You *knew*?' I asked.

Geoffrey froze. 'I knew they made plans to build a fence, but I thought it was nothing but talk. I never thought they'd go through with it. And I was too scared to check for myself if it was true.'

I searched his face while Joshua glared at him. 'But you seem to know so much.'

'Like I told you, I worked for the government as a scientist. When they began talking about building a fence, about separating the country, they wanted me to join them. But my family was already infected at

225

that point and I couldn't take them with me, so I decided to stay with them. I didn't know if I was infected myself. I never really thought we'd be deserted.'

'And the government just abandoned you?' Shock was obvious on Mom's face. How she could still be shocked about anything after what Tyler had just told us was a mystery to me.

'I knew too much. I guess they only let me live because they thought I wouldn't survive more than a few days in Weeper territory.'

Karen scowled at him. 'Why didn't you tell us any of this before?'

'I didn't really know what the truth was any more. I...' He swallowed. 'I was scared and worried too. Worried you'd hate me and cast me out. I'm sorry, it was selfish of me.' Nobody said a word and Geoffrey dropped his eyes and turned to Tyler. 'What else do you know, Tyler?'

'Oregon, California, Nevada and Arizona are restricted areas. The fence runs along the borders of the outer states and separates us from the rest of the country. From here, the nearest section of the fence is south of Las Vegas. You'd reach it in six hours by car.'

Joshua and I exchanged looks, and we both knew we wanted to see the fence with our own eyes.

Tyler looked straight at us, his eyes wide and pleading, as if he knew what we were thinking. 'You can't ever go there. They'll catch you and then it'll be over. You'll die. Just like my brother.'

'Your brother?' My mouth went dry, because I was sure another horror story was about to be added to my memory. Another thing I could never wipe from my mind.

226

Tyler traced the tattoo spelling his name on his wrist. 'My twin, Tyler. He died in the lab. He didn't make it out of there.'

Karen was the first who got over the shock that seemed to paralyse us. 'I'm sorry. But if Tyler was your twin, what's your name?'

Tyler rose and dusted himself off. It was like he was shutting down. 'It doesn't matter. That guy doesn't exist any more. Just call me Tyler.'

He walked into the house, leaving us with nothing but the certainty that everything was even worse than we'd thought.

Dad turned out the light, ignoring my protests. Izzy giggled. The glow of candles filled the room. Orange and yellow. They flickered, making shadows move on the walls.

'Happy birthday' surrounded me. Bobby sang off-key on purpose. Izzy tried to drown him out with her loud screech.

I was tempted to cover my ears. A grin spread on my face. All my friends were there. Except for Abi. She'd been sick for a few days. A virus, they said. Nobody was allowed to visit her in the hospital.

Mom put the birthday cake on the table. It was pink and blue and white. 'Make a wish.'

Twelve candles. Their glare dazzled me.

A wish.

That pair of pink Converse.

Or that Brittany got a bad case of acne.

Or…

Brown eyes flashed in my mind. Heat crept into my face.

I want Alex to like me as much as I like him.

Closing my eyes, I blew out the candles. Smoke wafted up my nose and my smile widened.

CHAPTER SIXTEEN

The next day, Karen and Larry waited for Joshua and me in the kitchen. I'd known something was wrong from the moment I'd visited Mom and Dad in the infirmary cottage that morning. They'd avoided looking me in the eye, as if there was something they felt guilty about.

'I think we should have a discussion about Safe-haven,' Karen said.

I'd suspected this conversation would come ever since Tyler had told us the truth. It had changed everything and made us realize that Safe-haven was even less of a safe place than we'd thought.

Joshua exchanged a worried look with me before he turned to Karen. 'What about it?'

Larry wrapped an arm around her. 'We think it would be better to leave the winery and search for a new place to stay.'

'We?' Joshua echoed.

'The adults had a conversation yesterday,' Larry said.

Joshua's expression tightened. He didn't like that nobody had asked us. *I* didn't like it either.

Karen put a hand on his shoulder but he shook her off. 'We agreed to move away.'

'But why?' I blurted out, horrified about the prospect of leaving our home.

'It's too dangerous to stay here. Tyler's words made us finally realize it. The Weepers know where we live and now the military does, too. I bet the helicopter had a camera. And maybe we could find more survivors during our search for a new place to

231

stay. We could join forces. That way we'd be less vulnerable,' Larry said.

They had made up their minds already.

'Isn't there another way? Safe-haven is our home.'

Larry shook his head. 'We must think of the future. Safe-haven is no longer a safe place.'

I didn't like it at all, but I knew they were right.

The military, or the government, or whoever was behind the fence, knew where we lived and they'd left us to die. They wouldn't hesitate to kill us if they thought we were a danger to their web of lies.

*   *   *

Everything was packed, except for the furniture. Larry had found and patched up an old trailer, so we could take the cows with us and wouldn't have to butcher them—their milk was more important than their meat.

It was strange to think that this was our last evening in the winery. We'd find a new Safe-haven, a new home, but I didn't want to leave. I loved the pretence of peace in the vineyard, this sense of another time. Of my other life.

I exchanged a smile with Karen while we set the table—the plates and cutlery barely fitted. Elbows on the tabletop would be a no-go during dinner. I'd forgiven them for making the decision about moving without us. Joshua, on the other hand, was still furious.

In fact, I'd sensed anger building in him ever since we'd found out about the fence. I could tell he felt betrayed that Geoffrey had kept it from him. And perhaps he felt stupid for ever allowing himself to trust a man who had helped to create the virus in the first place. But Joshua didn't seem to want to talk about it and I didn't push him. I didn't want to spoil our last day at Safe-haven.

Marie stirred tomato sauce in a huge pot. Almost every meal here contained tomatoes and red peppers. I hadn't gotten tired of it yet. 1,141 days without fresh vegetables made me hunger for them.

Marie had told me she'd harvest the potatoes tomorrow so we could take them with us to our new home—wherever that would be. We planned on staying close to the ocean. The adults didn't want to risk moving closer to the fence.

'Sherry, look!' Mia said in excitement. I turned to her. She held up a piece of paper with her first and last name written on it in block letters. She was beaming at me.

'Larry says I'm a fast learner!' She glanced at Larry, who sat across from her at the table. He gave me a grin. He'd been in teacher mode for a few days. While he'd tried to teach Emma how to count to five, he'd made Mia write her name and that of every member of Safe-haven. He loved teaching others, and with Mia and Emma he had two willing students. He'd suggested he could teach me and Bobby too, but we hadn't found the time. Not that Bobby and I were too keen on sitting down with textbooks.

Mom helped Dad towards a chair, supporting him with an arm around his waist. It was only the second time he'd gotten out of bed. His leg hadn't healed yet, but at least the swelling was down. He still couldn't put pressure on it, though. Our journey to a new safe haven would cost him every bit of strength.

With a groan, Dad plopped down on a chair and

wiped his forehead. Karen had told me he'd probably end up with a stiff leg like Larry. As long as he didn't get rabies, I could live with that. His fever and sweating worried me. Karen still hadn't said anything. But what if he was already turning into a Weeper, and she wasn't telling us because she knew there was nothing we could do?

Mom smiled at him before she turned to us. 'Can I help?' Her skin wasn't grey any more. It was pale, but at least she could no longer be mistaken for the living dead. Dad and Mom had gained some weight, though they were still too thin. I wished I didn't have to worry about them so much.

Karen shook her head and gestured at the set table. 'We're done. You can sit down.'

'Dinner!' Marie shouted. Seconds later Joshua entered the kitchen, Tyler and Rachel just behind. Only Geoffrey was missing. He'd been keeping to himself since yesterday.

Everyone took their seats, chairs scraping over the floor and plates clanking when someone hit them with their elbows. It was strange for me that Grandma was no longer with us. I sat down beside Joshua. He took my hand under the table and the ghost of a smile crossed his face. I smiled back. It came naturally when I was around him.

8 days since we'd rescued Rachel and Dad from the Weepers, and now that they were in better shape, we wouldn't postpone our departure any longer. This was the first time we'd all had dinner together and it would be the last around this table. I pushed the thought aside.

I was sandwiched between Joshua and Bobby, but I didn't mind. It felt like a big family gathering. Chaotic but wonderful. The scent of pasta and tomato sauce filled the kitchen, making my stomach growl. God, I was hungry. Joshua chuckled and winked at me. I punched his leg under the table and scowled at him for laughing at me. He tried to keep a straight face, but failed miserably. I rolled my eyes and looked away.

Dad was talking quietly with Larry. They got along well. It was good for Dad to have someone who distracted him from his sickness, but I couldn't stop thinking about it. Even now I could see that his temperature was up, from the sheen of sweat on his forehead. Karen looked at me and gave me a sympathetic smile. What if she was just waiting for the right moment to tell us the truth?

I tried not to think about the Weepers and Dad's fever, but at night those worries kept me awake. For now, I leaned back in my chair, trying to enjoy the atmosphere. I smiled when my eyes landed on Rachel.

She sat beside Tyler and talked to him animatedly. He seldom replied, had hardly talked since he'd told us about the fence, but he seemed to listen to her. She looked so much better than when I'd first seen her, but her screaming often woke us at night. Every member of our little group was haunted by memories of their past, but we never talked about it. The future was scary enough. We didn't need the past to worry about.

Geoffrey finally slunk into the kitchen, head bowed as he sat down. Joshua followed this with a frown. What had taken Geoffrey so long?

Karen sank down beside Larry, kissing his cheek with a soft smile. Marie put the pot on the table, before claiming the last free chair. She lifted Emma onto her lap and clapped her hands. 'Enjoy your meal!'

Everyone began filling their plates and started eating, the clinking of cutlery filling the kitchen. In such a moment, it was easy to forget what lay beyond the walls of Safe-haven. I noticed Joshua kept glancing at Geoffrey, who hadn't looked up once. I wondered what he was thinking.

After dinner most of the members of our patchwork family went upstairs to their rooms. Dad had to lean on Mom as they left the kitchen.

I watched them go. Only Geoffrey and Joshua stayed in the room with me.

'You shouldn't worry so much,' Joshua said.

'The fever still hasn't disappeared. Sometimes I think he'll never get better.'

'Karen is sure it's just because of the inflammation in his leg,' Joshua said, taking my hand again and squeezing it.

I gave him a small smile before I looked over at Geoffrey. 'And what do you think? You probably know the rabies better than all of us.'

Geoffrey folded his hands on the tabletop; they were trembling. 'Your father doesn't show any additional symptoms. The fever's even lessened to some degree. The other survivors with rabies showed excessive thirst and heightened aggressiveness. Your father shows none of those signs. The sweating worries me, but I don't think he's got rabies. His leg is just taking longer to heal because his body's still weak.'

The way he avoided my eyes made my stomach churn. But before I could respond, Joshua leaned forward, his arms propped on the table and eyes fixed on Geoffrey. 'Do you want to know what I find strange?' He didn't wait for Geoffrey to reply. 'We

236

all know why you're an expert on the virus, because you told us as soon as we met you: you helped create it. And that's got to be the very worst thing anyone could have to admit. And yet you were too "scared" to tell us what you knew about the fence…'

Geoffrey opened and closed his mouth and looked at both of us nervously.

'And when that helicopter flew over,' Joshua continued, his suspicions spilling over, 'knowing what you know, you must have realized it was pointless trying to get their attention, but you didn't stop me, did you? What if they'd shot at me? Or perhaps that wouldn't matter to you. Perhaps you're on their side! You worked for the government once—who's to say you ever stopped?'

I gasped. What was Joshua saying? Could it be true?

'He lied to us, Sherry,' Joshua hissed. 'We never should have trusted him!'

Geoffrey went pale, as if life had left his body. 'I never—'

Joshua interrupted him. 'I've kept an eye on you. Since Tyler started talking again, you've been acting weirdly. I guess he ruined your plan to keep us in the dark, right? You've probably done everything in your power to hide the truth from us.'

Geoffrey shook his head, looking panicked. 'I don't work for the government any more, I promise you!'

'Then what's going on with you?' I asked. 'Why *have* you been so quiet?'

He swallowed visibly. 'Tyler's words shocked me just like everyone else.' He paused, taking a deep breath. 'But they also got me thinking about something I heard before everything broke down and the government built the fence. It's been on my mind constantly…' He hesitated.

Joshua looked ready to explode.

'Just tell us!' I said.

'There were rumours of a cure.'

Whoa. What?

Joshua's eyes grew wide. 'A cure? What kind of cure?'

My mouth went dry. I wasn't sure I could have spoken if I'd tried.

Geoffrey's face was pleading. 'It was just a rumour and by that time I wasn't working on the rabies any more, so I don't have first-hand knowledge…but after what Tyler said about the labs and how they're testing something on humans, I started wondering if the rumours might be true after all.'

'What were the rumours?' I snapped.

'A few scientists in Washington had been working on a cure and immunization project. The government had asked them to do research, but I don't know if they succeeded or how far they even got with it,' Geoffrey whispered.

'But what if it's true? What if there's a cure?' Joshua said. A vein in his temple pulsed and his hands balled into fists.

Geoffrey let out a tired sigh and rubbed his eyes. 'If a cure exists, it's kept in one of the laboratories beyond the fence and we don't know anything about it. A cure still in development could be deadly, or even make the rabies worse.'

'But if there is one, perhaps it could heal the Weepers,' I said. 'And if Tyler told the truth, they are already testing it on humans, so it might work.'

Geoffrey looked sad when he shook his head. 'We don't know that. People died in those tests. Maybe

238

it isn't possible to give the Weepers their humanity back. Maybe they're lost for ever. Even if there is a cure, I don't know where the laboratories are. They could be anywhere—Tyler told me he doesn't remember where he was kept—and they'll be heavily guarded. You'd never get past the fence anyway. You'd risk your life for the minimal chance that there might be a cure.'

'Why didn't you mention this to anyone?' Joshua narrowed his eyes. 'Why did you pull back from us? You should have shared this with everyone straight away.'

Geoffrey fidgeted with the hem of his shirt. 'Look, I didn't say anything because I didn't want to get everyone's hopes up. Risking our lives by searching for something that probably isn't even there will only get us killed. I'm just trying to do what's best for our group.' His eyes were imploring. 'I know you're worried about your father, Sherry, but nothing can save him if he's infected. Don't chase after the impossible.'

I looked away. I felt drained. For a moment, I'd really thought there might be a way to help the Weepers, to give them their humanity back. Now the situation seemed just as hopeless as before. Yet somewhere in the back of my mind, the spark of excitement Geoffrey had kindled refused to die out.

'Excuse me, I'm tired.' Geoffrey rose from his chair and walked towards the door. He stopped and turned back to us. 'I'm sorry if you feel you can't trust me. But the truth is there's so much death on my conscience, I just can't take any more. And I knew if I told you about the fence—and the cure— you'd put yourselves in danger to find it. Don't do anything stupid, Joshua, and take care of Sherry.

The government won't hesitate to kill you if you try anything with the fence.' As if every movement cost more strength than he could spare, Geoffrey left the kitchen.

I glanced at Joshua, my mind racing. I could only hope he wasn't planning on getting over the fence by himself. The mines would blow him up, even if a bullet didn't bring him down first. He was used to doing things alone, but if he wanted to get to the other side, then he'd have to take me with him.

'Let's get out of here,' he said, grabbing my hand as he stood.

I raised my eyebrows.

'I need some fresh air.'

I let him pull me to my feet and followed him into the courtyard. We strolled towards the ivy-covered wall, our hands entwined. Joshua hoisted himself up with little effort and held his hand out to me. With his help and my own pathetic attempts, I climbed up next to him and plopped down. I moved closer to Joshua's warm body, pulled my legs against my chest and rested my chin on them.

We sat beside each other on the cool stone, facing towards the vineyard. The sun was setting over the hills and the chatter of birds filled the silence. Everything looked so peaceful—as if nothing had changed, as if the world hadn't turned deadly. It was strange to think that this was the last time I'd see the vineyard. I leaned my head on Joshua's shoulder and slipped my hand into his.

I tilted my head and glanced up at him. 'Maybe I'll try to get over the fence and search for that cure,' I said. Despite his warnings, Geoffrey's words had shown us a new chance to do good, to do more than search for food or hunt Weepers.

240

Joshua's face was unreadable, but at least he wasn't trying to talk me out of it.

'Geoffrey believes it's only a rumour. He doesn't think there's any hope,' I continued, hoping to get a reaction out of him.

'He doesn't think there's hope because he's lost everyone he really cared about. His wife and children are dead. Nothing, not even this cure, can bring them back. But we have people we care about, people we don't want to see die.'

Joshua's voice had risen to a shout. He let his head fall back and glared at the sky. 'You could get rabies, and then I'd have to watch you die like I watched all those people in the bunker die, and so many of the people I saved and brought here. I don't want to watch you die. I couldn't stand it.'

I sat up, startled by his words. 'I won't get it. Maybe I'm immune like you.' My voice was calm and collected. Inside, I wasn't calm at all. He wanted to get over the fence and search for a cure just as much as I did.

'If we got past that fence we could live a normal life. Maybe my father's still alive, maybe he's living on the other side.' Joshua ran a hand through his hair and let out a long breath. 'I just want to believe that there's a way to get there.'

I looked up at him. It seemed as if there was more he wanted to say, but he stayed silent.

'I know. I feel the same way.' We owed it to everyone. If it was rabies causing Dad's fever, I'd be able to save him. We could help so many people, maybe even give the Weepers their lives back.

Joshua's eyes were focused on the vineyard. 'I don't want to give up hope. I owe it to Zoe. What if the cure could help her?' His eyes fluttered shut and

241

my chest constricted at the sight of his pain.

Joshua shook his head as if to get rid of those thoughts and brought his face close to mine. Since that time in the vineyard when Bobby had interrupted us, we hadn't kissed. So much had been going on in Safe-haven that we hadn't found time alone. And kissing in front of the others was out of the question. Bobby had watched Joshua and me the entire time since he'd found us hugging. Even Mom and Marie looked at me with those unnerving, all-knowing expressions.

Joshua had stopped, his face centimetres away. Was he waiting for me to make the first move?

I leaned in and brushed my lips against his. Sweet and warm. Joshua wrapped his arms around me and pulled me closer. Our kiss was soft, and loosened the knot in my stomach.

When we pulled apart, I was breathless. Our faces were still close and his breath warmed me. From the corner of my eye I noticed movement, and I turned my face towards it.

Mia stood in the courtyard, shifting from foot to foot, watching us curiously. An image of her as a Weeper flashed into my mind, but I pushed it away. When she saw me looking her way, her face lit up. She dashed towards us and peered up the wall. 'Did you kiss?' Her small nose wrinkled in disgust.

'What did I tell you about being nosy?' I asked, raising my eyebrows.

'Don't do it.' She smiled sheepishly. 'Can I come up?'

I glanced at Joshua and he gave a nod. He kneeled on the edge of the wall and extended his arms. Mia stood on her tiptoes and he pulled her up, making her giggle. Smiling, I made myself comfortable, sitting cross-legged, Mia cuddled up to me, her head resting on my lap.

Joshua took his place beside me and I leaned my head on his shoulder. The sun had disappeared— only a soft glow illuminated the sky, tingeing it orange. In the distance, I could see Tyler and Rachel strolling through the vines. It was good that Tyler wasn't on his own any more. It must have been horrible for him to lose his twin.

I closed my eyes, breathing in the cool air while I stroked Mia's hair. Her breathing had become even and her body relaxed against mine.

'She reminds me of my sister,' Joshua said in a whisper.

I kissed him, my fingers tangling in his soft hair. Some of the tension left his body and the ghost of a smile crossed his lips.

As long as I still had my family and Joshua, I could survive in this scary world. We were still alive. We *wanted* to live. And I knew one day we'd find a way past the fence.